'Happy New  **murmured.**

Then, without warning, he bent his head and pressed his warm, firm lips to Holly's.

Heat flooded her. With a tiny moan she melted against him and felt his hands on her shoulders, drawing her closer to that huge, solid chest.

Then suddenly, without warning, his mouth wrenched away as he stepped back.

'Damn, Holly, I'm sorry,' he grated. 'I don't know what happened. I'm sorry. Forgive me.'

'There's nothing to forgive,' she said softly. 'Dan, it was only a kiss.'

But it hadn't only been a kiss, and they both knew it. . .

Caroline Anderson's nursing career was brought to an abrupt halt by a back injury, but her interest in medical things led her to work first as a medical secretary and then, after completing her teacher training, as a lecturer in Medical Office Practice to trainee medical secretaries. She lives in rural Suffolk with her husband, two daughters, mother and assorted animals.

Recent titles by the same author:

A VERY SPECIAL NEED
THE PERFECT WIFE AND MOTHER?
NOT HUSBAND MATERIAL!
IF YOU NEED ME. . .
THE IDEAL CHOICE
THE REAL FANTASY
ONE STEP AT A TIME
TENDER TOUCH

THAT FOREVER FEELING

BY
CAROLINE ANDERSON

MILLS & BOON®

First published in Great Britain 1998
Harlequin Mills & Boon Limited,
Eton House, 18-24 Paradise Road, Richmond, Surrey TW9 1SR

© Caroline Anderson 1998

ISBN 0 263 80637 5

Set in Times 10 on 11½ pt. by
Rowland Phototypesetting Limited
Bury St Edmunds, Suffolk

03-9802-45648-D

Printed and bound in Great Britain
by Mackays of Chatham PLC, Chatham

CHAPTER ONE

DAN stared down into the pale liquid swirling in the bottom of the glass. Twelve-year-old malt. What a waste. It might as well have been distilled water for all the difference it made. He swirled it again, then drained it regardless and set the glass down with a defeated smack. It wouldn't help. Nothing helped.

He wrapped his arms around his ribs just as the next coughing fit attacked him, then dropped his head back against the sofa cushions and sighed. He couldn't even sit in his favourite chair because the cat had nicked it again. Hell's teeth, he thought. New Year's Eve, and I have a cold I can't shift, no help and there's snow on the way.

Terrific.

His advert was out in the professional journals— again—but who was going to be looking at them over the Christmas period? Nobody.

Of course not. And who would want to bury themselves away in the wild and woolly depths of north Norfolk anyway? No one with any sense. He was just reaching for the bottle again when the phone rang. 'Ah, hell,' he groaned and, stretching out a long arm, he hooked the receiver up and tucked it under his ear.

'Elliott.'

'Um—I'm phoning in response to your advert for a locum.'

Dan jerked upright, gulped and coughed. 'Sorry—got

5

a cold. Could you run that by me again?'

Lord, her voice was gorgeous. Deep, soft, mellow—
it flowed round him like a river of silk, distracting him so
that he forgot to pay attention to what she was saying—
almost.

He coughed again so that she had to repeat herself
and then stared at the receiver, almost stupefied. 'You
want the job?' he said incredulously.

'Well—yes. That's why I'm ringing.'

There was an element of uncertainty in her voice now,
no doubt induced by his gormless telephone technique.
Sharpen up, you fool, he chastised himself, and groped
for the right words.

'Ah—that's wonderful. Um, do you want to come
for an interview or are you happy to start—when *can*
you start, by the way?'

'Well—now, really. I haven't got anything booked at
the moment—I've been doing locum work in Norwich
and I just hate the city bustle, but I couldn't find anything
else at the time.'

That sounded promising. 'There's no bustle here, I
can assure you,' he said drily. No bustle whatsoever.
That was what put them all off. 'In fact, it's so quiet
you can hear the snow fall.'

'Sounds wonderful,' she said in that soft, mellow,
slightly breathy voice that made his gut clench and his
loins heat and his pulse hammer. Damn. She probably
looked like the back end of a bus—with any luck. Not
that it mattered. She wouldn't look at him. Not now.
Not after what had happened—

'So, do you want to come and check me and the
practice out?'

'Sure. When would you want me to start?'

He gave a short huff of laughter that turned into a spasm of coughing. 'How about now?' he wheezed when he could speak again.

'You sound rough,' she said, her voice coloured with concern. He tried to remember when anyone had last been concerned about him—anyone who wasn't paid to be, that was—and failed.

He swallowed. 'Just a cold that's been doing the rounds. I can't shake it off.'

'Is it bronchitis?'

'Nah.'

'Are you sure? Have you taken your temperature?'

'Listen, little lady,' he said, mustering his authority, 'if I want a doctor I'll ask for one.'

'I thought you did,' she said with a chuckle, and he felt his mouth tug with the beginnings of a smile.

'Not for me. Now, about this interview—where are you?'

'Near Holt.'

He blinked. Six miles away from Wiventhorpe, that was all. 'How about coming over now?' he found himself saying, and then wondered if he'd totally lost his marbles.

'Now?' she said, her voice surprised.

'Well, perhaps tomorrow—or the next day. I expect you're busy with family.'

'Actually, no. I could come now. It's only five-thirty so I could be with you at six—if it's not inconvenient for you.'

He looked round. It wasn't that bad—and, anyway, this was his part of the house. The upstairs part was clean, tidy and ready to go, and the surgery was always tidy. He made sure of that. There was just the kitchen. . .

'Fine,' he agreed quickly, before she could change her mind, and gave her the directions. 'Um—what's your name, by the way?' he said, remembering just before he hung up that that basic fact had escaped his notice.

'Dr Blake—Holly.' She gave a self-conscious chuckle. 'I was born at Christmas—well, just after.'

'In that case, happy birthday, Holly Blake,' he found himself saying, sucked in by her cheerful good humour.

She laughed. 'Thank you, Dr Elliott. I'll see you in a minute.'

She hung up, and slowly, thoughtfully, he cradled the receiver. Holly. 'Hey, boys, mind your Ps and Qs, now,' he said in his best threatening tone, giving the sleeping dogs a steely glare. 'We're having company.'

Two tails thumped in unison and then were still again. The fire was lit. Why should they move?

He stepped over the dogs, stretching stiffly to ease the kinks out of his bad leg, and flexed his knee experimentally. Damn. It was twingeing again. Perhaps he did have a temperature. His ribs ached and his head was killing him, but that was par for the course. After a year of headaches one more was hardly remarkable.

He went through into the surgery, flicked on the lights and checked to make sure it was tidy. The magazines were straight, the chairs were neatly lined up—only a brightly coloured toy which had escaped from the toy-box and hidden under a table threatened the status quo.

He put it back where it belonged and checked the consulting rooms. Nothing out of place. Good.

The office was a bit hit and miss, but Julia was coming in the day after tomorrow and would set it to rights. Until then he'd just have to muddle through. He daren't interfere with her system—it was more than his life was worth.

He went into the kitchen which served both practice and home, and stacked the dirty dishes haphazardly in the dishwasher. Mrs Hodges would wince if she could see him, but she wasn't here and Holly would be, all too soon.

He propped his lean hips against the worktop. Holly. What a voice. Even the memory of it did strange things to his insides—strange, foolish things that he would do well to ignore.

Ruthlessly he went over to the mirror on the wall in the hall and pulled off his glasses—the heavily tinted ones that hid less than he would have liked—and forced himself to study his reflection.

The right hand side of his face he knew well. He'd had it, or a version of it, for thirty-four years. The left was a different story. From just under the thick, almost black hair that sprang untamed from his head, a jagged scar slashed down across his temple through his eye, over the shattered cheekbone and down to the corner of his mouth. Beside that scar were other, finer scars incurred in the rebuilding process that had tried to recreate his face. The eyelid had been torn and was a little heavy, and when he smiled—not often, these days—the left side of his mouth stayed stubbornly at half mast, giving him a drunken leer.

And yet, if he turned sideways, he looked the same as ever, ruggedly masculine, his features strong if a bit rough-hewn, his lips firm and just full enough to promise—what? And who would be interested in their promise?

He closed his eyes. So Holly had a voice that did incredible things to his insides.

So what? His face was just the start of his problems. More significant was the fact that he couldn't drive for at least two more years and had headaches that crazed him with pain, and his leg gave way from time to time and his ribs ached with the cold—

The doorbell rang, its sound shrill just over his head, and the dogs wuffed lazily from the fireside, too comfortable to move more than their heads.

'Some guard dogs you are,' he muttered and, cramming the concealing glasses back on his nose, he opened the door.

The greeting froze on his lips.

Back end of a bus? Not in this lifetime.

She was gorgeous—and she wanted his job. He forced a weak smile to his frozen lips and opened the door wider.

'Holly—Dr Blake?' he croaked. 'Come on in—I've just put the kettle on.'

Holly tipped her head back and looked up at the man standing in the doorway above her. He was tall, dark-haired, and with the light behind him he seemed to fill the doorway with a slightly menacing air that made her breath catch. For a long moment he stood there staring down at her, his eyes concealed by heavily tinted glasses so that his expression was impossible to read, and Holly felt her heart thump in her chest.

Then he spoke, stepping back as he did so to let her in, and the light caught the side of his face and cruelly illuminated the jagged scars.

As she stepped up into the hall she had to restrain

herself forcibly to stop her hand from coming out to touch that tortured flesh. What had happened to him to hurt him so badly? And why was he hiding behind the shades?

She met his eyes—or tried to. The dark tint hid his eyes from her, adding to the air of mystery, but his mouth had a sardonic twist that held a wealth of bitterness and discouragement. Despite that, she didn't fear him. There was nothing to fear. She wasn't sure how she knew that, but she did. He was a gentle man—gentle and kind and patient.

The only person he would be cruel to was himself.

'Dan Elliott,' he said gruffly, holding out a lean, strong hand. She shook it, not surprised to find it warm and hard and dry, the grip sure. His handshake fitted him. She couldn't bear limp, damp handshakes. She gripped his hand back and smiled.

'I'm Holly,' she said, refusing to stand on ceremony. She wasn't big on ceremony, and there was something about this man that made her realise he wasn't, either. Was it the old, much-loved jeans that gave him away, or the jumper with little woolly sheep all over it—an obvious handknit, courtesy of his mother, perhaps? She suppressed a smile.

Releasing her hand, he closed the front door and she looked round, conscious immediately of the warmth. Through an open door she could see the source—a black wood-burning stove with two dogs sprawled in front of it. The little mongrel was watching her, head up, ears tipped. The other, a bigger dog the colour of chocolate, was too comfy even to do that, contenting itself with opening one eye.

On a chair beyond the fire a huge ginger cat had taken

up residence in the centre of the cushion, curled into a loose ball, his head upside down and his chin sticking up in the air in a curiously trusting gesture.

Holly turned her smiling face to the man beside her and caught his brooding stare. 'You love animals, too. Our house is always full of them.'

He gave a brief snort. 'They seem to have arrived one way and another. The cat adopted me, I was given the chocolate horror as a puppy by a patient after my accident—I had to walk for physio, and a dog seemed the obvious companion. I certainly got plenty of exercise clearing up after him for the first few months. The mutt was another patient's—he was going to have to be re-homed when the patient went into a nursing home—'

'And of course you had to have him.'

He shrugged. 'If you've got one you might as well have two.'

'Or three, or four.' She grinned. 'My father's a vet. At any time we have several cats and dogs, the odd hedgehog in the spare bathroom recovering from a road accident, a couple of geese—the list is endless. And as if that wasn't bad enough he's into rare breeds so we have a small flock of sheep—oh, and of course there's usually a horse or two, recovering from surgery or under observation, and then there's the cow.'

'It doesn't sound as if you see much of him.'

Holly laughed. 'Oh, I do. When I was ten I decided if I wanted to see him I had to go with him so I spent hours in the car going on visits to farms and helping him with the animals.'

'So why aren't you a vet?'

She met his eyes, dimly visible through the dark

glasses. 'Because I wanted to work with people. Why aren't you a vet?'

He snorted. 'Because it was always expected that I would be a doctor. Anyway, I don't think I met a real vet until I moved up here. The vets in London where I was brought up treated overfed plutocratic Pekingese and the occasional goldfish. They wouldn't have known which end of a cow to avoid!'

Meeting the flickering, twisted grin, Holly chuckled. She liked this man. He had a sense of humour.

He held his hand out towards the open door of the cosy sitting room. 'Suppose I fill you in and tell you all about the job and what I'm actually looking for in a locum and then, if you think you'd be interested in taking it on, I'll show you round. It's residential, by the way—did I mention that in the ad? It has to be because I can't drive and so we operate strange surgery hours. Anyway, there's accommodation included as part of the package.'

'That could be handy,' she said, wondering why he couldn't drive. 'My parents aren't far away as the crow flies but the roads are a bit basic in the winter. It's better not to go out any more than you have to on them.'

He snorted. 'Tell me about it. Come on in—I should sit on the sofa or you'll be covered in cat hair.'

Limping slightly, he crossed to the chair and scooped up the ginger cat who squawked indignantly and then, as he sat down, curled up immediately on his lap. For a moment the room resonated with his purrs, then he settled back to sleep, content to ignore them all so long as he was left in peace.

Holly sank into the soft, welcoming cushions of the sofa and waited. Dr Elliott chewed his lip thoughtfully for a second as if he was considering his words carefully, then looked up at her. Despite the glasses she felt his eyes like twin lasers, scanning her, missing nothing.

'I had an accident last January—almost a year ago now. As a result I can't drive, and that makes visits tricky. My patients wanted me back, however, so I've worked out a system. Basically, until midnight and from six a.m. they come to me, and from midnight to six I go to them in a taxi. Day visits that are impossible to avoid I also use a taxi for but it's expensive, inefficient and, anyway, there's more work than one person can handle. There always was—that's why I had the accident.'

'Too tired to concentrate?'

He looked down at his hands, his face expressionless. 'I fell asleep at the wheel. The other member of the practice had left some months before and I was getting more and more tired. It's impossible to get a permanent partner in this part of the world, but even locums don't want to work here—too basic. They don't think they learn enough because we don't have a million clinics and they have to do some real work—trudging up farm tracks in two feet of snow is beyond them.'

He shrugged, dismissing locums—herself included, presumably—at a stroke. 'Anyway, we had a flu epidemic. I just fell asleep, hit a tree and rolled the car. I was in hospital for four months.'

'Four months?' Holly blinked. 'My God. You must have had some serious injuries.'

He shrugged. 'Femur, ribs, spleen—you name it.'

'Ouch. That must have been horrendous.'

He laughed, a hollow sound that made her soft heart ache. 'Not really. I forgot to mention the fractured skull.

It was three weeks before I regained consciousness. By that time they'd done most of the technical stuff and it was all down to me. All I had to do was heal.'

'Physio?' she said sympathetically.

He snorted. 'Just a bit. Still, it worked. I'm back on my feet—the only problem is I can't drive for at least two more years because I had convulsions in ITU and they don't know if it might recur.'

She frowned. 'Like epilepsy?'

'Something like that. I just have to wait. I haven't had one since, but only time will tell. In the meantime I've trained the patients to come to me.' He scratched the cat's ear and brought forth another torrent of purring, then continued, 'What I'm looking for in a locum is someone to take every other night between midnight and six, do all the day calls and normal surgery hours if possible. I'll run all the clinics, take morning and evening surgery and do the late night and early morning emergency sessions.'

That was quite a load, even for two, Holly thought. Not the number of patients so much as the relentless availability of the single-handed GP.

'So who's been helping you up to now?' she asked.

He gave a wry chuckle. 'Are you serious? I haven't had anyone since it started raining. The country only has any appeal while the sun shines.'

'It was shining today.'

'Not enough for them.'

'So you've been on your own for weeks?'

'Try months.'

No wonder he looked tired. She speculated about the glasses—to hide the bags under his eyes? Maybe it was nothing to do with the scarring. 'Do you have any outside cover for evenings or weekends ever?' she asked, appalled he should be working under such arduous conditions.

'Oh, yes—technically. One of the Holt practices covers every other weekend. The patients don't like seeing them, though, so they ring me anyway.'

'Would they see me?'

He grinned, only the right side of his mouth lifting. 'Oh, yes. The farmers'd be fighting to be at the front of the queue if they knew you were here. They've all got a weakness for a pretty face. Anyway, it wouldn't mean being disloyal if you were working here. That's the real problem—they're all so busy being loyal they're killing me!'

She joined in his laughter but her smile soon vanished as he bent over, clutching his ribs and coughing harshly.

'You are not well—you really aren't,' she said firmly as he subsided.

'I'm fine.'

'Let me listen to your chest.'

'No. I can listen to my own chest. It's clear. It's just a damn cold.'

She leant back and eyed him in resignation. 'Are you always this stubborn?' she asked mildly.

'Sometimes I'm *really* stubborn.'

'Just so I know where I stand.'

He met her eyes and his mouth twitched in a wry grin. 'I really am OK. I just need help.'

'OK. I'm here. Tell me when you want me to start.'

'Friday? That's the second of January—I'll let you have tomorrow off as it's a bank holiday.'

She grinned. 'Big of you. That's fine. You said there's accommodation?'

'Yes—come on, let's go and have a look round.'

He turfed the indignant cat off his lap and led the way across the hall and into a large and slightly chaotic kitchen. 'This serves both of us and the practice staff. It's sandwiched between the two areas, which is quite handy. Oh, by the way, I have a housekeeper who pops in every afternoon and cleans the house and makes an evening meal for me and whoever else is living here— unless you're vegetarian or have a special diet? I'm not sure she could cope with that.'

She shook her head. 'No, I'm not vegetarian and I'm not picky, either. I've grown up eating what was put in front of me and, frankly, it would be wonderful not to have to worry about cooking. It's not something I'm frantically good at.'

He chuckled. 'Nor me. I got the housekeeper because I couldn't stand the sight of another TV dinner, and the house was knee-deep in dog hair.'

He opened the door at the other side of the kitchen and led her through into a passage. It had a door marked TOILET at one end, and then another door off it that led through into a waiting room with an outside door to the front of the house. There was an office with a reception hatch, and three other doors besides the cloakroom— two consulting rooms and a treatment room which by the look of it was used for minor surgery.

'The house used to be two cottages, and they were knocked together by my predecessor. The second set of stairs was taken out, which is actually a pain otherwise the flat would be more self-contained. However, we manage.'

The consulting rooms were pleasant, facing down the garden with a view in the distance to the sea about two miles away, Dan told her. The garden was bleak and wintery but surprisingly tidy, the little she could see of it in the spill of light from the windows. She guessed that, apart from turning the dogs out into it, he hadn't had the time or the health to set foot in it the entire year, and yet it looked well tended. He must have a gardener, she decided, resting her forehead on the cool glass.

'It's pretty in the summer,' he said from right behind her, making her start just a little. He was so tall, so close, so—so much. She fought the urge to lean back just to find out if that chest felt as solid and welcoming as it looked in his reflection, but then he turned away.

'Come and see your rooms. You may change your mind.'

'I doubt it,' she disagreed, turning to follow him through the kitchen and up the steep, narrow stairs to the upper floor.

They had to step over the cat on the top step, his tail swishing over the edge. Glancing over the banisters she saw the overgrown chocolate puppy watching the tail with interest. Fun and games, she thought with a little smile, and then had to slam on her brakes because Dan Elliott had come to a halt in front of her and she'd been so busy woolgathering she hadn't even noticed.

'He tolerates the mutts,' Dan said, indicating the snooty cat.

'Teases, more like.'

Dan grinned. 'That too. Here, this is the bedroom.' He pushed open the door of a pretty little room with wonky walls and flowery curtains and a honey-coloured carpet. There was a bed against one wall, a chest of drawers and wardrobe against the other, and the window looked out across the village green to the church in the middle, floodlit to show off the pretty little tower with its castellated top.

It was a lovely room. She turned, a smile on her lips, but he was gone, up the corridor, opening the next door. 'Sitting room,' he told her tersely, and she wondered what she'd done wrong because his mood had changed—blackened, somehow, become defensive.

She raised an eyebrow silently and looked around. Like the bedroom, it had flowers and a honey-coloured carpet and looked out over the church, but there was another window to the back as well, overlooking the distant sea. An old flickering-flame effect electric fire stood against one wall with a rug in front of it, to give the illusion of a hearth, and the little suite was clustered round the rug. To one side of the fire was a television, and yet Holly couldn't imagine herself curled up here watching it.

It was cheerful and homely, cosy enough even with the central heating, but it lacked the warmth of Dan's sitting room. It lacked the dogs, the real fire, the lived-in, permanent feel of that slightly tired room downstairs, and she knew where she would rather spend her time.

'There's a bathroom at the top of the stairs—I've got my own off my room so you won't have to share.'

Holly wondered which of them would have been more worried about that, and decided it was him. She'd shared a bathroom with her parents, two brothers and a sister all her life. She was used to queueing and washing at twice the speed of light and not using too much hot water. Somehow she didn't think Dan was used to sharing anything, and she didn't think he wanted to. It made her feel inexplicably sad for him.

'Well?' he asked, his voice gruff.

'It's lovely,' she told him.

'It's adequate,' he corrected. 'So, Holly, do you think you could bear to work here?'

She looked up at him, so close to her in the narrow confines of the little corridor, and smiled. 'Oh, I expect I could tolerate it for a week or two,' she agreed.

He searched her eyes—at least, she assumed that was what he was doing. It was impossible to tell through those wretched shades, and she had an almost overwhelming urge to pull them off him and see what he was hiding from her. Then without a word he nodded shortly, turned on his heel and limped slowly down the stairs.

They went back into the sitting room and over a cup of coffee they agreed her salary, hours, starting date, when she would move and so on, and then just as he got up to see her out he had another coughing fit. This time he sagged against the wall, his arm wrapped tightly over his ribs, and swore vigorously between spasms.

'You have a chest infection,' she told him bluntly.

'I haven't,' he bit out, once he could speak again.

'You have. Let me listen to your chest. Where's your stethoscope?'

He glared at her, but she couldn't be bothered to argue. She'd seen one in the surgery and, without asking his permission, she went and retrieved it, cannoning into him on the way back through the consulting room doorway.

'What the hell do you think you're doing?' he growled, coughing again and turning away to lean against the wall.

She whipped the stethoscope up to her ears, hauled

up his jumper and slapped the frigid end onto the warm skin of his back.

He swore again, and she thought mildly that if nothing else she'd had her vocabulary expanded this evening. She listened to the crackling, scratching, bubbling noise of his chest and tugged the stethoscope back down round her neck.

'Did you say something about your spleen?' she asked bluntly.

'Hmm.'

'Are you on antibiotics prophylactically?'

He humphed again, and she sighed and slapped the instrument down on the desk. 'You have a chest infection. You need antibiotics, rest, warmth, fluids and sleep. You do not need to be working alone, handling cases probably half as sick as you are, when you should be in bed.'

She folded her arms and returned his glare. 'Do you have any antibiotics here or do I have to go and fetch some from my bag in the car?'

'I've got some,' he growled.

'So take them—now.'

He sighed roughly and stabbed his hands through his wild black hair, then turned on his heel and stomped away from her. 'Bloody interfering woman. Knew she was a mistake the moment I clapped eyes on her,' he muttered as he went.

She felt the smile tickle her lips, but held it at bay. One victory was enough, and she needed to save her big guns for the next salvo.

'I'm going home now for my things,' she told him. 'I'll be back in just over an hour. Don't go out unless it's life or death, OK?'

He turned, halfway up the stairs. 'No, it's bloody well not OK,' he snarled. 'Who the hell do you think you are?'

She smiled sweetly. 'Your guardian angel, of course. Now take your pills like a good boy and I'll see you soon.'

If there'd been anything on the stairs she was sure he would have thrown it at her. As it was she made her escape safely, ran to the car and jumped in before the chuckle broke free.

Interfering witch. Dan coughed again, his mangled ribs protesting violently, and with a muttered curse he dropped onto his bed, fumbled for the pills on the bedside table and swallowed one, followed by another just for good measure, then crawled back downstairs to the sitting room.

He flung a log on the fire, picked up the Scotch bottle, put it down again with a sigh and fetched a glass of orange juice from the fridge. She was right. He couldn't afford to neglect his health—too many people depended on him.

The sofa beckoned, and he sprawled across it with one leg up on the arm and the other bent at the knee, foot flat on the floor. The puppy came and laid against his foot, the cat settled along the length of his thigh and tortured the dog with his twitching tail. Dan took off his glasses, dropped them on the table and shut his eyes.

Ten minutes, he promised himself. Just ten minutes. . .

CHAPTER TWO

'You sure about this man?'

Holly looked up at her father's weatherbeaten, weary face and smiled. 'Yes, Dad, I'm sure. He's got two dogs and a cat.'

'So do lots of criminals and perverts.'

She laughed, but only softly. She knew why he was fussing. 'I'm sure he's fine. He's a bit of a growly bear, but he's just defensive. He's had some horrendous injuries.'

'I remember—it was in the paper last January. He nearly died. I seem to recall it took hours to free him, and the steering-wheel was buried in his chest.'

'Nice.' Holly winced inwardly. No wonder it hurt him to cough. 'He needs help, Dad,' she said quietly.

'Hmm. Well, you know where we are.'

She reached up and tugged him down, planting a loving kiss on his rough cheek. 'Thanks. Don't worry— I'm a big girl now, Dad. I'm twenty-nine.'

'Only just,' he growled.

She gave him an understanding smile. 'I really can cope, you know.'

He smiled bravely back at her, his concern still showing in his eyes. It must be hard, she thought, to see your little ones spread their wings—but she was fully fledged now, and the nest was getting just a tad cramped! She patted his cheek affectionately, gave him another quick hug and ran out to the car.

Her younger brother Richard had helped load it and was sitting in it with the engine running, warming it for her. He slid out from behind the wheel as she arrived, and went through a shorter version of her father's routine.

'You sure this guy's up front?'

'I'm sure.'

'Hmm. Keep taking the tablets, kid.'

She smacked him gently. 'He's going to be a colleague. It's a business arrangement. I've only just met him—and, besides, he's sick. If I'm going to have an affair, Rick, it'll be with someone with stamina!'

Her brother blushed, and then hugged her just a little too tight for comfort. 'Be careful,' he muttered, then posted her through the door, slammed it and stood back with a wave.

Her mother was out, down at the village hall preparing for the New Year's Eve party later. She would no doubt be on the phone the minute she'd heard what had happened, but there was nothing Holly could do and frankly she was quite happy without another 'are you sure' lecture!

She drove the few miles carefully because the weather was getting rougher, the wind picking up and the chill in the air more biting by the minute. There was that peculiar pale blackness that preceded snow, and Holly knew that they would wake to a white morning. She just hoped it would hold off long enough for her to arrive.

It did. She pulled her car onto the empty hardstanding in front of Dan's cottage, turned off the engine and opened the car door. The outside light was on, but there was no sign of Dan. She pulled her cases out of the car, carried them to the doorstep and rang the bell.

The dogs wuffed lazily, but still there was no response. Perhaps he was in the bath, she thought, and then just in case she tried the door.

It swung inwards, and with a sigh of relief she hauled her things inside, shut the door behind her and then looked up to see the two dogs watching her with interest. They were lined up in the sitting room doorway, heads cocked on one side and tails wagging, and beyond them she could see Dan stretched out on the sofa, one leg draped over the end, the other decorated with the big ginger cat, its tail for once hanging motionless as he slept.

They looked too comfortable to move so, after making sure the dogs remembered her, she took her things upstairs, came back down and put the kettle on, then went into the sitting room and perched on the edge of the chair.

He looked exhausted, she thought. Exhausted and ill. No wonder he'd jumped at her offer. He wasn't in a position to be picky about prospective locums. Anyone who could do the job even half competently must have seemed like a dream come true, and once he realised that she could cope he'd be able to relax properly— probably for the first time since before his accident.

He had taken off those dark glasses, and she studied the jagged scar that snaked across his temple and down over his cheek. With his eyes closed there was nothing to indicate why he might wear them, but perhaps the eye had lost its sight and wandered and he felt self-conscious. Who could tell?

She leant forward and laid her fingers gently on his wrist. It was a measure of his exhaustion that he didn't even stir as she took his pulse. Fast, of course, and he felt a little warm but, then, it was warm in here.

She went back to the kitchen, made a cup of tea and lifted her head, cocking it slightly to one side. Was that another doorbell? The dogs obviously thought so.

She went through to the surgery, flicking on lights as she went, and peered through the peephole. A large young man stood there with a nasty looking gash on his forehead, blood dribbling down into his eye.

She opened the door. 'Whatever happened to you?' she asked, reaching out to draw him into the surgery.

'Fell—just finished the milking and put the cows out, and I was hosing down the milking parlour and I tripped over the hose.'

'You drove yourself here?'

He grinned a little weakly. 'No—I live over there, just the other side of the church. I'm Mr Simpkin's stockman. Tried to clean it up myself, but looks to me like it needs stitches.'

'Hmm. What did you hit it on?' Holly asked, assessing the tetanus risk and also the advisability of stitching a dirty wound.

'Edge of the milk cooling tank.'

'Is it clean?'

He laughed. 'Should be. Milk all ends up in there. Yeah, it wasn't like it was all covered in cowsh—'

'No, I'm sure. When did you have your last tetanus booster?'

His grin was wry. 'Last year, I think, or the year before. That'll be in my notes. Are you a nurse?'

'No, a doctor—Dr Blake. I'm here to help Dr Elliott out for a while. And you are?'

'Joel Stephens.'

'Right. Come into the treatment room, Mr Stephens,

and let's find your notes and see if we can't get this head sorted out for you.'

She checked his tetanus status and, sure enough, he'd had a booster in March the year before for a puncture wound sustained on the farm. She swabbed the two-inch long gash, dried it off and looked at it critically. It should be easy enough to draw the edges together, and of course the sooner it was done the better the result. He was a good-looking lad. It would be a shame to let it mar his beauty!

She infiltrated the surrounding skin with lignocaine and adrenalin, waited five minutes which she spent usefully finding all the things she would need and then with her patient lying down on the couch, she slowly and painstakingly drew the edges of the wound together with a continuous running cosmetic suture. Finally she was happy and tied off the ends just under his hairline.

As she sighed and sat back she heard a slight sound behind her and turned to see Dan watching her through those wretched shades.

'Very neat,' he said approvingly.

She snipped the ends of the suture and arched a brow at him. 'Thanks.' She knew her tone was far from grateful, but she hated being patronised. Dan, however, was either too thick-skinned to notice her tone or too self-contained to react.

He shouldered himself away from the door and bent over the patient. 'Hi, Joel. In the wars again, I see.'

The lad grinned. 'Slipped in the cowshed. Lucky I didn't end up face down in the muck.' He shot Holly an apologetic glance. 'Thanks for sortin' me out, Doc.'

She gave him the benefit of her professional smile. 'My pleasure, Mr Stephens. Just make sure that you don't enjoy yourself too liberally tonight, mind. I don't want to hear you've been in the pub, swilling beer till three in the morning!'

He grinned weakly. 'You guessed!' he said with a chuckle.

She shook her head in resignation, sent him on his way with a smile and a dressing over the wound and cleared up her bits and pieces while Dan lounged against the wall and watched her silently. 'That was a neat job,' he said finally, breaking the silence at last.

'So you said.'

'You could have woken me.'

'Why?' she asked, turning, one eyebrow raised . 'So you could mess up his face because you're too tired and too ill to see straight?'

His neck went an interesting shade of brick, and he mumbled something that could have been an apology. She turned away, hiding a smile, and gave him the benefit of the doubt.

'Fancy a cup of tea?' she asked, extending the olive branch. 'I've put the kettle on.'

'I'll make it. Are you hungry?'

She suddenly realised she was—starving, and she hadn't eaten for hours. 'I am, actually. What did you have in mind?'

'Mrs Hodges left a casserole. Rice OK with it?'

'Fine. Thanks. I'll be through in a minute.'

She hid another smile, surprised at the little hint of domesticity hitherto disguised. She needn't have been surprised. When she joined him in the kitchen a few minutes later it was to see two bags bobbing gently in the boiling water.

'Boil in the bag rice?' she said innocently.

'You got a problem with that?' he growled, and she stifled her chuckle.

'No. Love it. I lived on it at college.'

She picked up the cup of tea that he shoved towards her and cradled it in her hands, watching him over the rim. 'Are you feeling better for your snooze?'

'Yes—thank you.' His voice was curt, but she ignored him.

'You looked wiped. I really didn't want to wake you.'

He flushed again, as if it was somehow a weakness to have been caught napping. Perhaps he felt vulnerable, knowing she had watched him sleep. She offered him a conciliatory smile. 'You needed it—when did you last sleep through the night?'

He glowered. 'I have no idea.'

'Precisely. I'll take any calls that come in overnight and during tomorrow so that you can get back on your feet again before surgery starts properly on Friday—OK?'

'It isn't really necessary for you to be here at all,' he grumbled. 'Not that I don't appreciate the help—don't get me wrong—but I could have coped.'

Holly smiled and just about avoided patting him on the arm. 'Of course you could,' she soothed, which earned her a narrow-eyed look. She lifted the lid on the other pot and sniffed appreciatively. Mrs Hodges was worth her weight in gold, she thought, her stomach rumbling agreement. If every day was going to end on a high note like this she could learn to live with it!

Her little suite of rooms was cosy, comfortable and very welcoming—which was just as well, as it was the last thing that could be said about Dan. After they'd finished their evening meal and shared the clearing up she made them both a coffee.

If she'd cherished any illusions about being invited into his sitting room to drink it he despatched them instantly.

'I'll see you in the morning,' he told her. 'Feel free to wake me if you need anything you can't find.'

And he went into his sitting room, shut the door with a quiet but decisive click and left her standing there, cup in hand, staring open-mouthed at the door. Oh, well, she thought, and with a philosophical shrug she went upstairs and unpacked her things, putting them carefully away before going into the sitting room and turning on the television.

New Year's Eve, she thought, and here I am on my own, covering for an ungrateful, bad-tempered man with all the grace of a cornered crocodile, and I'm doing it by choice!

She would have laughed if she hadn't felt so lonely. Then she reminded herself briskly that she was there because he needed her, however prickly he might be, and her resentment faded. Poor man. He'd been struggling alone for so long and here she was, complaining because she had to do it for five minutes!

The trouble was that she was never alone, and wasn't used to it. There'd been a time when she'd thought she'd love it, but she'd discovered through the lonely times when she'd been working too hard to make friends and had been too tired for a social life that the undemanding presence of family was something precious that she hadn't appreciated. Just someone to smile, to hand you a cup of tea, to tousle your hair, however irritating it was—she'd missed it, and she wondered what it was like to live alone always as Dan did.

No wonder he had the dogs!

She heard them wuff, heard the faint echo of a door-bell, and slipped her feet back into her shoes, before running downstairs.

Dan was just heading through the kitchen towards the surgery when she caught up with him.

'Excuse me, my job!' she said with a grin.

'But—'

'But nothing,' she said, firmly pushing him aside and nipping in front to open the surgery door.

The woman waiting there with the child in her arms looked a little taken aback at the rather crowded wel-come. She looked blankly at Holly for a second, then smiled at Dan over her head.

'Hello, Dr Elliott,' she said tentatively. 'I wonder if you could just listen to Becky's chest. She's been cough-ing and coughing all evening. I thought she'd settled but it's much worse now I've put her to bed.'

'Of course—come in, Mrs Rudge.'

Dan laid an apparently gentle hand on Holly's shoul-der and propelled her firmly out of the way so the woman could get in, then led her into the waiting room. 'This is Dr Blake, by the way,' he told the woman. 'She's going to be helping me out for a while.'

Mrs Rudge gave Holly a distracted smile. 'Hello,' she said briefly, and then turned her eyes back to Dan, sink-ing down onto a chair and settling the little girl on her lap. 'She's been almost choking—as if she couldn't get her breath. There, look, she's starting now.'

The child—about five years old Holly guessed—started to cough, her chest bubbling away, then sucked in air with a great whooping noise. As they watched she seemed to reach a point where the air was lodged in her lungs and she simply couldn't shift it to breathe out.

She started to gasp and without thinking Holly snatched her from her mother's lap and squeezed her chest, releasing a rush of air. The child started to breathe again, the cough started up again, and yet again there was a whoop and Holly had to press the little girl's chest wall to release the air.

'Dan, put the kettle on,' she said without looking up.

'I have,' he told her, crouching down beside them. 'Well, Becky, I think you might have whooping cough, my love. Has she been immunised?'

Mrs Rudge nodded. 'Yes. Oh, yes, as a baby. They all were.'

'Well, I'm glad because she's got it quite severely.'

'How can she if she's been vaccinated?'

'Easily—but without the vaccine she would have been much worse. Come into the kitchen.'

They all trooped through into the other room, where the kettle was just coming to the boil, and while Holly settled the woman and child at the kitchen table Dan poured boiling water into a bowl, put it inside the washing up bowl to prevent accidental scalding and tipped a few drops of Olbas oil onto the water.

Immediately the scents of menthol and eucalyptus filled the room, and he put the bowl down on the table beside the mother and child, draped a big towel over the child's head and the bowl and told Becky to breathe nice and steadily.

She coughed again a moment later, but without the terrible jamming of her breath, and at last she seemed to be shifting some of the mucus that blocked her little lungs.

While she sat under the towel Holly made them all a cup of tea and settled down at the other side of the table to watch Dan in action. He was in his shades, of course, propped against the worktop, his jeans snug on his lean hips. He was actually a very attractive man, Holly realised with surprise, and wondered what he would look like if he took off the glasses and smiled a real, proper smile.

Now, however, he wasn't smiling but watching and listening to their young patient. 'Does she ever vomit?' he asked the mother.

'Sometimes, when she's coughed a lot.'

'Well, keep an eye on it. I think you're going to have to sleep with her so you can help her if she stops breathing after a coughing fit in the night—she's not likely to come to any harm, but she may well panic if she's fighting for breath. It's very scary for little ones.'

'It's pretty scary for their parents,' Mrs Rudge told him with a shaky laugh.

'Yes, I know.' He put a hand on her shoulder and squeezed gently, and the woman smiled up at him with obvious affection and respect. 'Don't worry,' he assured her, 'we won't let any harm come to Becky. She'll be fine. You just need to keep her out of draughts, away from smoke—and that includes an open fire as well as cigarettes—and steam her several times a day to help shift the junk off her chest.'

'With that smelly stuff?'

'Ideally. Have you got any?'

She shook her head and Dan handed her the bottle. 'Take this, then. I've got more. If she vomits very often let me know because she really should go to hospital if that's the case. Try and get plenty of fluids into her, anyway, and lots of little light meals, rather than three big ones, so her stomach doesn't have too much to cope with. OK?'

He lifted the towel away from Becky's head and grinned down at her. 'OK, tiddlywink?'

She smiled at him, her wan little face flushed from the steam, and nodded. 'I can't breathe sometimes,' she told him.

'I know. Still, you'll be all right. Mummy knows what to do, and we're just here if you need us.'

Her trusting little face shone up at him, and Holly felt rather than saw the ache that went through him. He lifted the little girl up and gave her a hug, then handed her back to her mother. 'Take her home and keep her indoors. Changes of air are as bad as anything. Hang a wet towel over her bedroom radiator at night and keep the heating on if you can. If she needs to see me again I'll come to her to save her going out in the cold again.'

'I didn't like to ask,' Mrs Rudge explained.

Holly intervened. 'I'm here now and I've got a car. I can come at any time of the day or night,' she told her reassuringly. 'Just ring.'

The young mother nodded, and they saw her out to the car and then locked the surgery door and went back into the kitchen. No doubt, Holly thought, he'll go back in that cosy sitting room and I'll go back to mine and stare at the blank walls and wonder why I'm doing this—'

'Fancy a drink?'

She almost refused. She'd hardly finished a cup of tea ten seconds before. Then she thought about that lonely room upstairs, and turned to him with a smile.

'OK. I'll put the kettle on.'

He gave a wry grin. 'I had in mind a glass of malt whisky—to see the new year in?'

Holly glanced at her watch. It was ten to twelve. She returned the grin. 'OK—but a very small one. I might have to drive later. And you shouldn't, really, not with the antibiotics.'

He sighed. 'Do you ever stop fretting?' he asked mildly.

'No. I'll pour them.'

'I was afraid of that,' he said, taking down two small shot glasses from the cupboard over the sink. 'Come on.'

He led her through into the sitting room, and she perched on the sofa with her scant dribble of whisky and ruffled the ears of the chocolate dog that came and leant against her, tongue lolling.

'What is he?' she asked curiously, studying the dog.

'Guess.'

'Well, it's chocolate Labrador coloured, but that's all. Build-wise and facially it's a border collie. It's a chocolate collie!' The dog grinned at her, pleased by her analysis, and she rumpled the soft thick fur and looked at Dan. 'Am I right?'

He nodded. 'Mum was a Lab called Kahlua after the chocolate liqueur, Dad was a neighbour's sheepdog who sneaked out for a bit of the other. Buttons was the prettiest, I was told.'

'Is that his name—Buttons?'

Dan nodded, and she chuckled. 'Does that make you Prince Charming?' she asked, and got the giggles at the very thought.

He glowered at her. 'Very funny,' he growled.

'Well, at least we agree!'

He sighed and crossed over to the window, pushing

the curtain aside and staring out into the night. 'Why did I take you on?'

'Because you need help—and because you realised what an asset I was going to be to the practice,' she said cheerfully. 'And, anyway, I was here and nobody else was. Did anybody else apply?'

He shook his head. Holly grinned. 'There you are, then. It was meant. I'm local, I know the roads like the back of my hand and I'm not going to whinge if it snows.'

'It's snowing now,' he told her.

She jumped up and went over to him, peering through the gap in the curtains. 'So it is,' she breathed. 'I love to watch it fall.'

'So do I. It looks so innocuous. Funny how deceptive it can be.'

As Holly stood there watching the snowflakes drift and melt against the windowpane, she suddenly became aware of how close he was to her and how large he was, even against her far from insubstantial frame. He topped her by a good six to eight inches, and his shoulders were massively wide. She could smell soap and whisky and something more basic, a subtle masculine aroma that did peculiar things to her insides and made her suddenly, desperately aware of that big, virile body so close to hers.

And then the clock on the church struck midnight, and in the distance they heard cheering and car horns hooting at the pub across the green.

Dan dropped the curtain and looked down at her, his expression masked by the glasses. 'Happy New Year, Holly,' he murmured, and then, without warning, he bent his head and pressed his warm, firm lips to hers.

Heat flooded her. With a tiny moan she melted against him and after a second's hesitation she felt his hands on her shoulders, drawing her closer to that huge, solid chest.

Her palms flattened against it, and beneath them she could feel the steady thudding of his heart. Her own heart was racing, thrashing against her ribs, and she could feel her legs trembling as if they would give way.

She leaned into him for support and then, with a ragged groan, his hands cupped her head, steadying it as he deepened the kiss. Her lips parted to the searching sweep of his tongue, and she felt the sharp, clean edge of his teeth against her lips. He nipped her gently, then sucked the tiny wound, driving her crazy with need.

Forgetting herself, forgetting everything, she slid her hands up and tunnelled her fingers through his soft, thick hair, holding him closer. One of his hands slid down to cup her firm bottom and lift her against him, and with the shock of awareness she felt the hard ridge of his desire against her aching body.

Her cry was lost in his mouth, trapped by the wild mating of their lips and tongues, and then his hand was cupping her breast, gently squeezing the soft fullness. She arched against him with a gasp, and then suddenly, without warning, his hand was gone, his mouth wrenched away as he stepped back.

She would have fallen if he hadn't reached out and steadied her. Dimly, her eyes soft-focussed, she watched him staring at her in horror as he backed away.

'Damn, Holly, I'm sorry,' he grated. His voice was rough, his breath rasping, and a dark flush lay over his cheeks. She wished she could see his eyes, see what he was feeling, work out what had happened.

He turned away, thrusting the curtain aside and resting his forehead against the cool glass. Gradually his breathing steadied, the harsh sound giving way to the hiss of the fire and the purring of the cat. Then he lifted his head and turned to look at her, and even with the glasses on she could see the anguish on his face.

'I don't know what happened. I'm sorry. Forgive me.'

'There's nothing to forgive,' she said softly. 'Dan, it was only a kiss.'

But it hadn't been only a kiss, and they both knew it. He turned away, throwing another log on the fire, and finally she made her feet move.

'I think I'll go on up to bed,' she said in a strangled voice. 'Is the phone switched through to my room?'

'I'll do it.' His voice was gruff, still not his own. 'You're sure about taking tonight?'

'Of course. Don't forget your antibiotics.'

He gave a choked laugh. 'I wouldn't dare,' he said wryly.

She went towards the door, but just before she passed through it his voice stopped her.

'Holly?'

She turned back to him but his expression was unreadable. 'Yes?'

'It won't happen again.'

She regarded him steadily for a moment, then smiled—a little sadly. 'How did I know you were going to say that?' she murmured, and, turning on her heel, she ran lightly up the stairs, went into her bedroom and shut the door. Her body still ached and thrummed, her lips were full and puffy and her arms felt extraordinarily empty.

She crawled into bed, closed her eyes and wished she wasn't there alone.

CHAPTER THREE

DAN dropped into his chair and buried his face in his hands. His mouth felt tender and swollen, and he could still taste Holly, sweet and clean like nectar on his lips. He groaned at the memory of her soft, ripe breast in his hand, the feel of her body firm and slim and athletic and yet soft, so soft. . .

His body still yearned for her, and he shifted a little to ease the tension on his jeans. Damn. How could it have happened? One minute they were standing there, looking out at the snow, the next he was groping her like a randy adolescent behind the school bikesheds!

And her eyes—gorgeous blue eyes like cornflowers against the healthy outdoor glow of her skin—had been wide open and unfocussed, their invitation clear. Her hair, blonde and silky, had been scraped back into a simple ponytail with one of those gathered fabric bands, and he had been almost overwhelmed by the urge to pull the band off and sift those silken strands through his fingers. It was long—long enough to fall like a curtain over her breasts, hiding their lushness from him—

'Damn!'

He stood up sharply—too sharply. His leg crumpled and he sagged against the arm of the chair with a gasp of pain and a string of words that should have made even the cat blush.

Buttons pushed his wet nose into Dan's hand and

whimpered softly. Dan rubbed the floppy ears affectionately while he got his breath back and stared down into
the mournful, pleading eyes of the hopeful youngster.
He hadn't walked them all day and guilt stabbed at him.

He gave him another affectionate pat. 'No, boy, I
can't, I'm sorry. Not tonight. I'll stick you out in the
garden for a minute. Come and see the snow. Rusty,
come on.'

The other dog was already at the door with his tail
lashing, expecting their usual walk, but it was more than
Dan could cope with. His chest was killing him, his ribs
ached, his leg was giving him stick and his head was
pounding. Instead he pulled on a jacket, opened the back
door and went out into the quiet night.

The dogs ran around, tails up and noses down, sniffing
at the snow that was just starting to settle on the grass.
Buttons, meeting it for the first time, bounded round
trying to bite the fat, heavy flakes as they fell. Dan let
them play for a while. The cat joined them only for as
long as was necessary, treating the snow with great
disdain and dashing back inside as soon as he had
relieved himself. He was far too mature to play with the
nasty, chilly stuff!

Dan smiled. They were good company, he thought.
There'd been times when without his animals he thought
he would have gone insane—and others, of course,
when he thought they would drive him insane, but that
was natural and Buttons was bigger now and hopefully
over the worst. He'd destroyed a waste-paper basket and
one leg of the kitchen table would never be the same
again, but otherwise he'd been a very easy dog to
bring up.

Thank God. He didn't have time to deal with a

difficult dog. Just fitting in their two walks a day was complicated enough, and there had been days when only one walk had been possible, and that had been a short one.

Ah, well. They could be a lot worse off than with him, Dan supposed. He whistled softly and they came bounding up to him over the snow, ears flying, tails lashing, tongues lolling.

Why were they always so unfailingly cheerful? Or should he ask the other question? Why was he always so unfailingly cheerless? He closed the door and turned the key. He knew why he was cheerless. Part of the answer lay with the constant, nagging ache from his injuries and the never-ending pressure of work.

The rest of the answer, the more complicated part, lay in London in a smart townhouse overlooking Regent's Park, just walking distance from the Harley Street clinic he had been groomed for all his life.

Pity his father had forgotten to consult him, really, or he could have saved all of them a great deal of pain and frustration.

And talking of frustration, he thought as he stood in the kitchen, he could hear Holly's bed creaking right overhead, and immediately his senses were clamouring again for a sweetly scented woman with long blonde hair and cornflower blue eyes and the softest breasts he had ever felt in his life. . .

It was a quiet night. The only call was at a quarter to six, and Holly was glad to get up and end the pretence of sleeping. She had lain on her back, staring at the ceiling and listening to Dan coughing all night and she was only too happy when the phone rang and she could legitimately make her escape. She pulled on her clothes, ran lightly downstairs and pulled on her boots and coat, before letting herself quietly out into the moonlit early morning.

The snow had been falling all night, but it had stopped now and the sky was clear. The temperature had plummeted, and Holly hoped the roads were gritted by now because she was in a hurry.

A young man had been taking his wife to the hospital to have her baby and had been unable to get the car off the drive because of the snow. While he'd struggled to clear it she had proceeded to rush through her labour with unseemly haste and Holly knew from his description of events that she had only a very short while to cover the two miles to their cottage if she was to arrive before the baby.

Luckily her car had four-wheel drive, as did most of the cars her family owned. Living where they did and doing what they did it was almost essential. Holly cleared the windscreen, swiped the majority of the snow off the bonnet and jumped in, backed out of the drive and turned carefully onto the road.

Her headlights cut through the curiously bright night, making yellow beams over the cold blue-white of the moonlit landscape. Under any other circumstances she would have stopped to admire it. Now she just concentrated on getting there safely to deliver a baby that was clearly coming with or without her permission.

On the man's advice she parked at the top of the drive, a steep slope that led down to a pretty brick and flint cottage so typical of Norfolk. Lights were on upstairs and down, and as she slammed the car door the front door was yanked open and she heard the piercing cry of a new baby.

Well, it's alive, she thought as she retrieved her bag from the back seat and, making her way carefully down the drive, she greeted the young man who had phoned her.

'Hi. How is everything?'

'Fine, I think, but I'm extremely glad to see you. Come in.' He looked shell-shocked, she thought. His eyes were bright, his cheeks were flushed over a ghastly pallor and he looked in need of urgent first aid. His wife, on the other hand, lying in state on the three piece suite with the squalling baby draped over her now-soft abdomen, looked calm and relaxed.

'Hello, Doctor. Sorry to drag you out like this. The midwife was out on another call.'

'My pleasure.' She put her bag down and shrugged off her coat, then turned back the towel covering the baby. At first glance everything looked fine. 'Could I wash my hands?' she asked the man, and he showed her through to the kitchen.

'Shall I put the kettle on?' he asked. 'You'll want hot water, won't you?'

She laughed. 'You've been watching too many films. By all means put the kettle on—I'm sure we could all do with a cup of tea—but all I need to sort your wife out is a clean bowl with some warm water, a fresh flannel and towel and a bar of soap—OK?'

He looked relieved. Holly left him busy with her instructions, but before his wife had anything to drink she just wanted to make sure that the placenta was intact and there was no danger of haemorrhage.

Everything, in fact, looked fine. The young woman,

whose name was Gill Partridge, had produced the baby with a minimum of fuss and within moments was happily suckling it while Holly tidied her up, washed her and put in a couple of little stitches where she had a tiny perineal tear.

It was an hour later when Holly left, content that everything was well and that the woman didn't, in fact, need to go to hospital as her husband was now on holiday, and made her way back to Dan's cottage, starving and ready for a nice big cooked breakfast to warm her up.

As she pulled onto the drive the front door was yanked open in a flurry of snow and he stepped out onto the path, his brows knitted together. 'Stay there. We've got an emergency. I'm coming.'

So much for breakfast. She turned the car round, and seconds later the door opened and Dan jumped in.

'Go!' he instructed.

She just looked at him. 'Which way?' she asked mildly.

He bit off an oath and pointed in the opposite direction to the one from which she had come. 'Elderly man, chest pain. His wife can't get a lot of sense out of him other than that. I've called an ambulance.'

'When did she ring?'

'About ten minutes ago. Why didn't you take the mobile?'

'What mobile?' she asked, shooting him a withering look. 'You didn't tell me about a mobile.'

'I would have given it to you when the first call came in, but by the time I'd realised you were going out you'd gone.'

She sighed. 'I think we're going to have to sit down

and talk about this more extensively,' she said. 'For instance, why are you here now and not just sending me?'

'Because I know him.'

'You know all of them.'

'Not like this one. He's got Alzheimer's, and he doesn't even recognise his wife.'

'So why does he need you?' she asked with irrefutable logic.

'Because she does,' he replied. 'I'm coming for her sake, not his. Left here.'

He said nothing about her driving but his knuckles were white, and when the car lost traction slightly on a bend his legs braced against the floor hard enough to poke a hole in it.

'Relax,' she soothed.

He snorted. 'It's hard to relax when you know just how damned easy it is to almost kill yourself on these roads. I don't relish another four hours being cut free from a wreck.'

'I thought you were unconscious?' she asked, puzzled.

'Not, unfortunately, at that point. Turn right up that lane, then pull over outside the second cottage.'

It was a little cottage, very like the other one she had just visited only this one was seeing in the new year in a very different way.

They pulled up outside and went to the door, and as it swung open Holly had a fleeting glimpse of a tiny, grey-haired woman who fell sobbing into Dan's open arms.

It was too late to do anything for her husband. He had apparently had another heart attack shortly after she had phoned, and had gone straight away.

'I know it's silly,' she said a while later, wringing a handkerchief and staring at the body of her husband slumped in the chair, 'but I'll miss the cantankerous old bugger.'

'I know you will,' Dan said gently. 'You were wonderful with him, Mrs Gray. Everyone else would have given up.'

'At least I don't have to feel guilty,' she said tremulously.

'No. No, you have no need to feel guilty at all.'

The ambulance arrived at that moment, and Mrs Gray watched them remove her husband's body in dry-eyed silence. Then, when the doors had closed and it had driven away, she sagged against Dan and wept again.

'Are your family coming over? Have you told them?' he asked her.

She nodded 'Yes. I rang my daughter just before you got here. They're on their way, but the children are still asleep and it'll take them a while to get here from King's Lynn.'

'What about a neighbour?' he was asking as there was a knock on the door.

Holly opened it, to find a man and woman standing there in coats over their nightclothes. 'Is everything all right?' they asked. 'We're next door—we saw the ambulance and we wondered—'

'Oh, Letty, it's Tom,' the old lady said, and the couple came in and wrapped their arms round her and hugged her as she began to sob again. The woman turned to them.

'We'll look after her. You go on if you need to.'

'Her family are coming,' Dan told them.

The woman nodded. 'Thank you, Dr Elliott. I'll keep

an eye on her and bring her to you if she needs anything.'

'Do. Thank you, Mrs Franks.'

They trudged back to the car and drove home in silence. As they arrived Dan turned to her with a weary smile. 'Thanks for the lift.'

'My pleasure.'

They went in and he reached for the kettle to put it on. 'Tea?' he offered. It was her third cup of the day, but she needed it.

'Lovely,' she said. She tugged off her boots, sat down at the table and ruffled the dogs' ears.

'So, where was your first call to?'

'Oh, Gill Partridge had her baby.'

'She did? It's early.'

'Mmm. Ten days. It was fine—a girl. No problems.'

'Sutures?'

'Two—mainly for cosmetic purposes. Nothing substantial. No, they're all fine. Her husband looked a bit stunned.'

Dan chuckled. 'He would. He's a solicitor. Delivering babies isn't part of his brief.'

She shared his laughter, then caught his eyes through those damnable shades and felt the laughter jam in her throat. Was it really only eight hours since he'd kissed her? It felt like for ever, and yet she could still feel the imprint of his lips on hers. She looked away, conscious of the heat flushing her cheeks, and turned her attention back to the dogs, just in time to see Buttons disappear round the door with one of her boots hanging from his jaws.

'Buttons! Bring that back here this minute!' she ordered. There was a scurrying noise, and she chased him into the sitting room and behind the sofa, then back out and into the kitchen and all round the table before Dan finally headed him off, demanded the boot back and scolded him for being a naughty dog.

Then he chucked both dogs out in the garden for a few minutes and turned back to Holly with her boot.

'Sorry about that.'

Somehow the game with Buttons had broken the ice between them. She took the boot and looked up at him, and for the first time she realised he was actually smiling as if he meant it.

It transformed his rather hard, angular face, and made him even more devastatingly attractive. Not that he needed to be. He was already more man than she knew what to do with.

'Thanks,' she said a little breathlessly, and put the boot with the other one out of Buttons's reach. 'How about some breakfast?' she said, casting around for a safe topic. 'I'm ravenous. Fancy something cooked if there's anything around?'

'Sounds good. There are all sorts of things in the fridge.'

She opened it and fossicked about in the contents for a minute, coming out with eggs, bacon, sausages, mushrooms, tomatoes and even a couple of cold boiled potatoes to slice and fry.

'Good grief,' Dan murmured.

'I did mean a proper breakfast,' she threw over her shoulder with a grin. 'It's the only meal I can cook. Do you want to put the kettle on and make some fresh tea or coffee and cut some bread while I do this?'

Then, having put him to work, she bustled about scrambling and frying and grilling and within minutes they were sitting down to steaming plates piled high with fragrant and delicious goodies.

'Oh, wow, I haven't had a decent cooked breakfast in years,' Dan said around a mouthful, and attacked his plate like a man possessed.

Holly, smiling to herself, followed suit just a little more delicately. Eventually she put her knife and fork down, pushed her empty plate away and sat back with a sigh.

'Yum,' she said with satisfaction.

'Yum, indeed. I don't think I've ever seen anyone so skinny eat so much so fast.'

She laughed at his astonished expression. 'I always did have a good appetite. Do you want to change the rules now you realise what you're feeding here?'

He chuckled. 'Not at all. It's a pleasure to see a woman who doesn't fiddle with her food.'

And that, she thought, was a loaded remark. She could feel her mouth getting all ready to be inquisitive when the phone rang and saved her—or possibly him—from herself.

'Dr Elliott's practice,' she said, and at the sound of her mother's voice she relaxed, hooked the chair over towards the phone and sat down on it back to front, her arms resting on the back. 'Oh, hi, Mum. Happy New Year to you, too. How was the party?'

'Fine. We missed you. Are you all right?'

'Yes, fine. We've just had breakfast.'

'One of yours?'

Holly chuckled. 'Yes, one of mine—and yes, he's still conscious.'

Dan shot her a quizzical look and she grinned and flapped a hand at him, telling him not to worry. Then her mother changed tack, and she was profoundly glad that Dan was on the other side of the room and couldn't hear what she was saying.

'Look, darling, about Dan Elliott. I was talking to Mabel Blanchard last night, and she remembers his ex-wife—did you know he's divorced?'

'No, I didn't.'

'Yes—only a couple of years ago, but I gather the marriage was over long before then. She's lived in London almost all the time he's been here—snooty creature, according to Mabel, and without a scrap of warmth. The word is that he's very quiet, keeps himself to himself, no social life that anyone's heard about—rather a recluse, from what I could gather, and a bit morose. I just thought you ought to know so you can be a little wary. He may be fine, but it's possible he's got emotional problems and I know what a sucker you are for that sort of thing. Just be careful, OK?'

'Yes, Mummy,' she said dutifully, which earned her a good-natured ticking off.

'I mean it, darling,' her mother added quietly. 'He's had a dreadful time for the past few years, by all accounts. It may have affected him. He may not be quite balanced.'

Holly shot Dan a searching look. 'He's fine, Mum. I'll speak to you soon. Love to all.'

She hung up and met Dan's eyes. 'My mother,' she said unnecessarily. 'She wanted to warn me about you.'

'Me?' he said, astonished.

'Mmm. Says you're divorced and don't have a social life and might not be quite safe to be around. I think she's afraid you'll do something unspeakable to me.'

Then Holly thought of the kiss, and the unspeakable things she'd spent the night wishing he was doing to her, and wished she'd kept her mouth shut.

He searched her eyes for a moment then looked away with a strained laugh. 'Wise woman, your mother. I ought to meet her and thank her for trying to pass on a little common sense to you.'

'I have plenty of common sense,' Holly said indignantly.

'Do you? So why don't you use it to keep out of my way?'

'Do you want me to?' she asked after a moment.

He stood up, his chair scraping on the kitchen floor. 'No. And that's the problem. What I want and what's right are two quite different things. Let's just use your mother's advice to make sure you don't come to any harm.'

He was walking to the door when Holly's next words stopped him in his tracks.

'Did your ex-wife fiddle with her food?'

He froze, then turned towards her, his eyes hidden by the damn glasses. 'Yes—just like you fiddle with things that aren't your concern. Butt out, Holly. I don't need you—even if I want you. Just bear that in mind.'

And with that he strode out, whistled for the dogs and went out into the freezing air, still dragging on his coat.

Holly sat on the chair, resting her chin on the back, and stared after him. '*Even if I want you.*' A surge of something hot and powerful washed through her. Was this it? The elusive X-factor which had been missing from her previous relationships and which had therefore kept them all platonic? The mystery ingredient without which she had felt obliged to hold back from commitment?

Her lips tingled with the memory of his kiss, and if she thought about the hard, warm feel of his hand against her breast she'd go insane. She watched him through the window as he walked the dogs down the hill towards the church, over the village green towards the pond.

He was limping slightly, the cold probably affecting his broken leg, and he was out in the raw air without a scarf over his mouth. It wouldn't do his chest any good, she thought, and told herself not to fret. He was in his mid-thirties, for goodness' sake! He didn't need a nanny!

Even if I want you. Dear God, she thought, how can I cope with this? Working with him, living with him, was going to be next to impossible unless she could manage to persuade herself to ignore the crazy things he did to her mind—and body—every time he was in sight or earshot.

Blinkers and earplugs, she decided. With a sigh she got up and cleared the breakfast things away into the dishwasher, wiped down the table and went into the surgery. As she was going to be working with him—at least until he told her to get lost—she might as well acquaint herself with the filing system and discover where all the forms and bits of vital equipment were kept so she could put her hand on them when she needed them.

She'd done locum work for two years now, and was very used to going into new places and making herself at home. That meant, of course, that the task she'd set herself took very little time, and so she was almost glad when the phone rang.

'Hello. Surgery,' she said cheerfully.

'Oh. Um, is Daniel there?'

A woman—older? 'No, I'm sorry, he's not,' Holly told her. 'Can I get him to call you?'

'Yes, thank you. It's his mother. I'm just ringing to wish him a happy New Year. Perhaps you'd be kind enough to pass it on.'

'Sure. Of course. He's just walking the dogs.'

'Right.' There was a meaningful pause, then Dan's mother said, 'Um—I don't believe we've spoken before.'

Holly hid the smile she knew would show in her voice. 'No, I don't believe we have. I'm his new locum—Holly Blake.'

'Oh.'

Did Holly imagine the wealth of disappointment in Dan's mother's voice? Had she hoped that Holly's presence might indicate an interest in the opposite sex? Holly could have enlightened her, but she didn't think it was her place to tell the woman that they were on the same side!

Having promised again to pass the message on, Holly replaced the receiver and went upstairs to her rooms. The snow was gorgeous now that the sun was out, and she wanted to take some photographs before it all got too trampled.

She found her camera in her bedroom and looked out of her window to see if there were any spectacular shots to be had from there.

There were, but not of the snow.

Dan was coming back with the dogs still bouncing beside him, and in the glorious morning sun they made a lovely picture. She snapped off two shots, before closing her window and going downstairs to put the kettle on.

She heard the door go and Dan's sharp command to the dogs which stopped them running through into the sitting room covered in snow and sent them instead straight in to her.

She fielded them with the skill born of years of practice, settled them down on their beds and turned to Dan with a smile. 'Coffee?'

He looked a little taken aback and uncomfortable. Was he still chewing over their conversation? Probably. She slid the coffee across the worktop to him, took hers over to the table and sat down, nursing the mug between her hands and watching him casually.

'Your mother rang—she said, "Happy New Year".' Holly doodled in a dribble of coffee on the table. 'She wanted to know who I was—I think I disappointed her.'

He snorted. 'I don't doubt it. She's itching for me to have an affair with someone.'

Holly sipped her coffee and said nothing. She got the feeling it wasn't just his mother itching, but as he was clearly trying to avoid picking her up and using her to scratch the itch she thought it politic to keep quiet. Dan, obviously regretting saying as much as he had, dropped into a chair, hooked another one towards him and propped his big feet on it.

He was wearing tweedy woollen socks, the sort that her father wore under his wellies in the winter, and she felt suddenly very much at home, sitting there in the kitchen with Dan with the dogs sprawled nearby and the cat washing himself on the window sill.

How cosily domestic, she thought.

The same thought must have occurred to Dan because he dropped his feet to the floor, picked up his mug and went towards the surgery door. 'You wanted to have a chat about procedures,' he reminded her, and the intimate and cosy moment was banished.

Just as well, she thought. It would be all too easy to talk herself into letting him use her to scratch that itch, and she had rather more planned for herself than that. She followed him, emulating his brisk manner, and found she agreed with the way he did most things.

There was nothing strange or untoward about his practice, nothing she hadn't encountered before or had a problem with, and—provided he would allow himself to stand back and keep out of the way and let her carry her part of the load—there was no reason why their relationship shouldn't be successful.

Their professional relationship, that was. Their personal relationship was a totally different matter entirely and one Holly was going to have to give some considerable thought.

There was a part of her that wanted to run screaming from a man who was half crippled, reeling in the aftermath of a cold and bitter marriage and now showing all the emotional warmth of a hermit.

Another—and, Holly was afraid, much larger and more dominant—part wanted to wrap him in her warmth and drive out the ice in his heart. Her head screamed 'Danger!', but her heart went conveniently deaf.

He was a good man, a kind man, caring and generous, and a blind man on a galloping horse could see he was hurting inside. He just needed love and understanding, Holly thought, and she was beginning to get the sneaking feeling that she might be just the person to give it to him. . .

CHAPTER FOUR

THE patients' bodies didn't seem to realise it was a public holiday. Holly, dividing her time between dealing with the patients who came to the practice and answering calls to those unable to get out, wondered how she had ever thought working in the country would be peaceful!

At least Dan seemed to be getting some rest, though. His cough still worried her, but on her insistence he spent the next few hours by the fire with the dogs, sipping hot drinks and generally unwinding.

Once it dawned on him that he was able to trust her he started to relax properly and actually slept for a good part of the day. Holly, popping her head round the door from time to time, found the sight of his long, rangy body relaxed in sleep more unsettling than it had any right to be. She was drawn to him like a moth to a flame, and realised that she was spending far longer than she should, hovering around him.

Weak-willed, she scolded herself. In a quiet moment she took the dogs for a short walk round the green, and bumped into Joel Stephens, the stockman from Church Farm, on his way back from feeding the young stock. She eyed his grubby dressing with disapproval.

'That'll get infected if you don't keep it clean,' she told him.

He grinned. 'I spent hours leaning up against the side of the cows milking them earlier, and since then it's been the calves. Course it's grubby. I'll go in and change it now.'

'Why don't you pop over to the surgery and I'll do it? I'd like to see how it looks today anyway.'

He nodded. 'Just let me finish up here and I'll be with you. Ten minutes?'

'Fine.' She gave him a wave and headed back, with the dogs bouncing at her heels. Giving in to the urge, she ran with them across the green and back to the cottage. As they all tumbled through the door they were greeted by Dan, bleary-eyed and without shades, standing in the kitchen talking on the phone.

He turned away from her and reached for the sun-glasses tucked in his shirt pocket, but she put her hand on his and held it down. He couldn't argue and, anyway, he needed the hand to jot down the message. Instead he turned away again.

As he put down the phone and reached again for the glasses Holly spoke, groping carefully for the right words.

'Dan, don't,' she said softly. 'You don't need them just because I'm here.'

'Who says?'

'I do.'

'And you are—?'

She sighed. 'OK, so my opinion doesn't matter. I just didn't want you to feel it was necessary just because I was around.'

'Why don't you just admit to being curious and have done with it?'

She laughed. 'Curious? The only thing I'm curious about is the colour of your eyes.'

He snorted. 'Grey. And, trust me, Holly, you

don't want to see. It's not a pretty sight.'

She put the kettle on for something to do to stop her going to him and taking him in her arms. If he got much prettier he might not be safe with her! 'Dan, I've seen you without them while you were asleep. It doesn't matter.'

'It matters to me,' he said tightly.

She gave up and crossed over to him, reaching up and touching the torn and damaged flesh—her palm curling against the cheek he had turned away from her. 'It shouldn't,' she said gently.

He didn't flinch from her touch, but she could tell by the coiled stillness of his body that it was unwelcome. After a long moment he removed her hand, his fingers gripping hers almost painfully. 'I don't need your pity or your professional counselling skills, Dr Blake,' he said through gritted teeth.

'I wasn't offering you either. I was simply suggesting that in your own home you ought to be able to be comfortable.'

'Maybe I'm comfortable with the glasses on,' he retorted.

She eased her hand away from his, surreptitiously massaging her crushed fingers. 'Maybe, but I doubt it. If you were you wouldn't take them off every chance you get.'

'If you didn't sneak up on me every chance you got it wouldn't matter, would it?' he growled softly.

Holly sighed impatiently. 'Dan, I don't sneak up on you.'

'Of course not.' He let out a slow breath and, turning, he met her eyes. 'There. Have a good look. Satisfy your curiosity, little cat.'

She did, seeing his eyes properly for the first time. They were the most lovely deep, mottled blue-grey, and they reminded her of the granite bed of a mountain stream. And right now they looked every bit as hard.

'You've got beautiful eyes,' she whispered. 'It seems such a shame to hide them.'

They locked with hers, and for an instant they softened, showing a deep, yearning ache. Then the softness vanished, driven out by the granite hardness of his resolve, and he unfolded the sunglasses and put them on. 'Back off, Holly,' he warned.

She stepped back and turned away with a quiet sigh. 'Have it your own way.'

'I will,' Dan said, his voice tight. 'Joel's coming up the path, by the way. Did you know he was coming?'

'Yes. I'm going to change his dressing and check his wound.'

'Good idea. His is not a clean job.'

She went through to the surgery without another word, opened the door to Joel and forced a smile. 'Hi, again. Come on through.'

She led him into the treatment room, peeled off the dressing and cleaned up the skin again where a little smudge of dirt had crept inside the bandage. The wound looked good, and Holly was pleased with her needlework. She redressed it and sent Joel on his way with a few replacement dressings and instructions to pop back if there was any reddening or soreness in the area over the next few days.

Then she went back into the kitchen and found it empty. Dan's sitting room door was firmly shut, the television on, and if he'd written LEAVE ME ALONE on

the door in letters ten feet high his message couldn't
have been more obvious.

Well, it was her own fault. She'd interfered when
she'd been warned, pushed her luck and trampled all
over his sensitive feelings. What did she expect? He
was entitled to deal with his disfigurement in his own
way. Why did she have to try and make everything right
with the world all the time?

With a bitter sigh she made a cup of tea and took it
upstairs. She was starving and it was now long past
lunchtime, but Dan hadn't mentioned lunch and, frankly,
she wasn't knocking on that damn door unless the house
was on fire! She sat down in front of the blank television
screen, turned on the lights on the fire to give a sem-
blance of cheer and stared blindly out of the window.

She could have been at home with her family, sitting
down to a huge roast lunch that would go on all afternoon. She could have been out on his calls with her
father, laughing and passing the time as they drove along
the lanes, or playing Scrabble with her brothers and
beating them hands down, or helping her mother piece
together another patchwork quilt.

Instead, she was upstairs in Dan Elliott's cottage,
staring into space and wondering where she'd left
her brain.

Dan glared at the dogs lying asleep in front of the wood-
burner. Damn them, how could they be so relaxed? He
was wound tighter than a coiled spring, and it was all
her fault. If only she would leave him alone!

His hand crept up to his face, touching the place
where she had laid her palm so gently against him. His
eyes slid shut, and an almost visceral ache filled him.

It had been so long since a woman had touched him—reached out and caressed him with such infinite tenderness.

The ache intensified and focussed into a physical longing to mesh with her softness, to lose his body in hers and forget, just for a while, the awful pain and loneliness and frustration of the past few bitter years. He dropped his head back with a groan and stared at the ceiling.

They'd missed lunch and he was starving now, but he hardly dared open the door in case she was in the kitchen. He didn't think he could trust himself not to grab her if she came within reach, and if she touched him again, however innocently—well, there was no way he could rely on his restraint.

He gave a humourless huff of laughter. Restraint? Where she was concerned? He'd already proved he had precious little, and he'd used that up last night, stopping the kiss in its tracks, when for two pins he'd have steered her to the settee and finished what they'd started.

No, he had no restraint where she was concerned.

The phone rang, and moments later he heard her soft footfall on the stairs and a light tap on the door. 'Dan?'

He jammed on his glasses and opened the door, gripping the knob like a lifeline. 'Yes?'

'I have to go out—a call. Have you got the mobile? It's some way and it's getting dark and starting to freeze again—'

'I'll come, too.'

'There's no need—'

'You shouldn't be out there alone—'

'Dan, back off! I don't need a keeper. I just want the mobile phone.'

He looked down into her stubborn, determined little face and knew he would never forgive himself if anything happened to her and he wasn't there to help her.

'I'm coming,' he said flatly and whistling for the dogs, he put them out briefly in the garden, pulled on his coat and gloves, picked up the mobile phone and checked the battery, then looked at her again. Her mouth was pulled into a tight line, her blue eyes were shooting sparks and she looked absolutely beautiful. Damn.

'Let's go,' he growled.

Holly was frustrated beyond belief. 'There's no need to snarl at me,' she said tightly. 'It was your idea to come, not mine. I don't need you here.'

'Let's get on with it. Where's the call to?'

She gave him the address and with a muttered curse he turned back from the door, pulled off his shoes and put on wellingtons. 'You'll need more than those little boots,' he told her tersely. 'It's a good mile up the track, the snow-plough won't have cleared it and if the farmer hasn't we'll have to walk.'

Holly frowned a little. 'But the snow isn't that deep.'

'It's very windswept there. They have a lot of drifting across the track. Who are you going to see?'

She sat down, tugged off her little boots and reached for her wellies. 'Jeremiah Sproat.'

'Old man Sproat? What's the problem?'

'Apparently he's just feeling generally unwell, but his daughter-in-law was a bit concerned about his colour.'

'Colour?'

Holly stood up and stamped into her wellies. 'She just said he looked odd.'

'Odd. Great. I'll bring my bag.'

Holly went out into the freezing dusk and noted with

dismay that it had started snowing again. Blast. That
was all she needed, although a fresh layer of powder
snow over the ice might give more grip. She chewed
her lip. The place they were going to was near her
parents'; perhaps it would be a good idea to go and
commandeer the Discovery. It had the best traction and
might well make it all the way up the track, even with
drifts.

The car door opened and Dan slid in beside her, his
long legs jutting towards the gear lever. She hoped he
wouldn't think she was groping him if she got his knee
by accident. She still felt foolish about touching his
face, but actions couldn't be undone. With her impulsive
nature she'd had cause to regret that on more than one
occasion.

'I want to go to my parents and pick up a Land
Rover,' she told Dan, swinging carefully out of the drive.
'They're only a couple of miles from the Sproats', and
it could save valuable time if there are drifts.'

He nodded. 'Good idea. Will they mind?'

She laughed. 'Shouldn't think so. I've been borrowing
cars for the last twelve years, off and on. They're
used to it.'

She turned into her parents' drive some twenty
minutes later, and found the farmyard full of cars. Surprise, surprise. Oh, well.

'Stay here,' she told him, 'it'll be quicker.'

She ran inside, hugged all her family and wished them
a happy New Year, collared her father and wheedled
the keys of his Discovery out of his pocket.

'Don't keep it overnight if you can help it because I'm
on call tomorrow morning and I might need it myself.'

She nodded. 'OK. Anything you want out of the back?'

He shook his head. 'Bring it back and come and join us for a bite on your way through.'

Right on queue her stomach rumbled. 'Done,' she said with a grin, and dropping a kiss on his cheek, she ran for the door, collected Dan and chucked her bag into the other car.

Dan swung himself up beside her and raised an enquiring brow. 'No problem?'

She laughed. 'Of course not. My father indulges me.'

Dan, eyeing her laughing eyes and flying hair, could see why. No man could resist her or deny her. He sighed and looked away, staring out across the cold, bleak landscape. It was snowing harder now, the weather closing in and settling down for a truly awful night.

As they turned up the farm drive a few minutes later he wondered what was wrong with old man Sproat and whether they would need to bring him out and send him to hospital. Then the car slithered in the snow and with a muttered curse he grabbed the handle in front of him and hung on.

'Sorry,' Holly said cheerfully.

Dan willed his fingers to release the grab handle and leant back in the seat. The car was tough, they were going at no speed at all and she was a competent driver.

He was still sweating.

Jeremiah Sproat had a touch of pneumonia on top of a chronic smoker's cough and the general debility of the very old. According to the notes, he was ninety-nine and would be getting his telegram from the Queen in a couple of months.

Holly didn't doubt that he would either, despite the pneumonia, because he was a tough old cookie with the lively intelligence of a much younger man. It showed in his sparkling eyes and quick words, although both were a little dulled by his condition. She remembered him from years ago, when she had visited the farm with her father and old Jeremiah had still been working. He'd been ancient then, she'd thought. In truth, he probably hadn't aged that much at all in the past twelve or so years.

Now, though, he was definitely under the weather. His colour, which Mrs Sproat had been so concerned about, was certainly a little odd, a chalky grey with the bluish tinge of anoxia and livid spots of colour on his cheekbones. He was a little feverish, and Holly could hear the gurgling of congestion in his lungs. He was short of breath and coughing up nasty stuff spotted with blood—partly, Holly thought, because of the lingering pall of cigarette smoke that hung like mist across the room.

She gave him a lecture on smoking, which rendered him temporarily stone deaf, and some antibiotics to start him off, handed the daughter-in-law a prescription for the rest of the course, repeated her lecture to her and retrieved Dan from the farm office where he was being swamped with details of the genealogy of the prize dairy herd.

John Sproat eyed her thoughtfully. 'Don't I know you, young lady?'

She smiled, her heart sinking. 'Yes. I'm Phillip Blake's daughter.'

'Thought I'd seen you—been a while, though. You'd have been a good bit younger.'

'Much. It must be nearly twelve years. Well, I'm sorry we can't stop and chat but we've got another call to make, and I'm afraid it's urgent.' She smiled again. 'Sorry. Dr Elliott?'

He was right there with her. 'Coming. Sorry to cut it short, Mr Sproat. Sounds as though you have a fine herd there. Happy New Year to you.'

They shot out of the door, dived into the car and Dan sighed. 'Phew. Thank God we've got another call. Where to?'

She flashed him a grin. 'My parents. They're feeding us.'

He sat bolt upright. 'What?'

'It's fine,' she soothed. 'We have to take the car back, anyway.'

'But what if we're needed?'

'We've got the mobile. People can ring.'

She kept her eyes on the road, but even so she could feel his eyes boring disapproving holes into her. 'I didn't realise we were going out for supper. I'm hardly dressed for it.'

She laughed. 'This is my family we're talking about and, anyway, it's not supper. They're all slopping around in jeans and sweatshirts and—if I know Mum—we'll be in the drawing room eating mountains of sandwiches and mince pies off our knees with the dogs lolling hopefully in reach of anything we drop and the cats trying to steal the cream off the tea trolley. Trust me, you are fine just as you are.'

More than fine. She kept catching sight of those lean, rangy thighs on the edge of her vision, and it took a real effort of will to keep her hands on the steering-wheel. For Dan's part, he subsided in a grumbling heap and muttered under his breath for a moment then fell silent, to Holly's relief. She hoped he wouldn't be too ungracious with her family. She loved them all very dearly and she wouldn't tolerate him picking on them. She considered threatening him, and then thought better of it. He was big enough to know how to behave.

She needn't have worried. They arrived back at her parents' house without mishap, and she parked her father's car, transferred their things back to her car and led a clearly reluctant Dan into the house.

The kitchen was deserted, with the exception of a cat curled up asleep on a pile of neatly folded washing. They followed the sounds of hilarity through the house, and behind her Holly could feel Dan's steps growing more and more hesitant. With a flash of insight she realised what had caused his reluctance, and her compassion rose to the surface again.

She turned back to him, resting a hand on his arm. 'Look, these people are my family. I can guarantee none of them will be armed.'

His mouth twisted in a wry smile. 'Sorry. I don't go out much any more.'

'You should,' she told him and, without allowing him any further concession, she pushed open the drawing room door and went in. 'Hi, guys. Have you left us anything?'

Dan wanted to crawl into a corner and hide. He knew it was ridiculous. He could cope with his patients on a one-to-one basis but a room full of people, all watching him and assessing him because their precious Holly was working with him and living with him, was more than he could stomach.

He managed a small smile. God knows what it looked

like. Forced, of course. He hoped he didn't look as ungracious as he felt. He sensed Holly's mother's eyes on him and turned towards her, seated beside him on the creaky old chesterfield.

'Are they prescription lenses?' she asked him.

He considered lying for a moment and then with an inward sigh he shook his head. 'No. No, they're just ordinary sunglasses.'

'Do you need to wear them?' she asked softly. 'I hate it when I can't see the expression in a person's eyes.'

Like mother, like daughter, he thought sourly. He could have taken them off because he knew she just wanted to study him and make sure her daughter was safe, and he couldn't fault her motives.

However, he wouldn't. Enough was enough for one day. 'I get headaches without them,' he told her. 'I had a fractured skull.'

Which was not really anything to do with the light, especially not in the soft lighting of the Blakes' drawing room! Mrs Blake's eyes searched his for a long time through the dark glass and then she smiled and patted his hand, as if she saw far more than the reflection of the Christmas tree lights on the front of the lenses. 'Let me get you something else to eat—how about some of my Christmas cake?'

He hated being understood, so easily read by a total stranger. He took the hefty slab of Christmas cake from her and picked at it almost angrily while she turned her attention to the others for a moment. Then the sofa beside him dipped again and Holly appeared on the edge of his vision.

'OK?' she asked very quietly.

'I'll survive, I guess. I feel like a goldfish in a bowl.'

She laughed softly, the sound rippling round him and through him—soothing and yet disturbing at the same time. 'Don't be silly. They just want to make sure I'm safe.'

'Mmm—like a pack of Rottweilers.'

She chuckled and stole a bit of his cake. 'Mum quizzing you about the glasses?'

'Said she liked to be able to see the expression in people's eyes.'

Holly grinned. 'You could have taken them off, you know. The Mafia look is very off-putting.'

'And would that help my case with the Rottweilers?' he asked wryly.

'Of course. They wouldn't want their little sister shacked up with the Mafia.'

He nearly choked on a crumb. 'Shacked up?' he spluttered when he could speak again. 'We're professional colleagues—'

'Mmm. I told them that.'

'And?'

She shrugged. 'They gave me that "Yeah, yeah, tell it to the fairies" look.'

Dan sighed and put the plate down on his lap. He thought another mouthful would choke him.

Holly pounced on it. 'Finished?'

'Mmm.'

'Good. I'll eat it. I love Mum's Christmas cake.' Her neat, even white teeth bit into the cake and a little crumb lodged on the edge of her lip. Her tongue flicked out to capture it, and he just caught the groan before it reached his throat. As he looked up her two brothers on the other side of the room were watching him steadily, and he got the feeling that he might just as well have groaned aloud for all the difference it would have made.

They knew just how he felt about their little sister—and they didn't like it one bit. . .

He was spared any further sparring with the Rottweilers because the mobile rang and Holly lobbed him the phone as her mouth was full of cake. It was Mrs Rudge, the woman with the young daughter with whooping cough, and she said Becky had started to vomit after every bout of coughing.

'Is she getting dehydrated?' Dan asked.

'I don't know. How do I tell?'

'Pick up the skin on her hand—if it stays up when you let go she's dehydrated.'

'Hang on—oh, yes, it does, quite badly. Oh, dear. What does that mean?'

Dan flicked a glance at Holly, who was laughing at something her father had said. 'It means we're coming over now and we'll have a look at her and decide what course to take then. Just hang on, we won't be long.'

Dan ended the call and looked up at Holly again. She was watching him now.

'Becky?' she said.

He nodded. 'Sorry. We're going to have to go—'

'I could drive you—then Holly could stay here for a bit longer.'

It was the younger Rottweiler, itching for a little chew on his jugular vein. Holly cut him off at the ankles.

'Thanks for the offer, Rick, but actually it's me that's on call, not Dan, so it wouldn't help.' She stood up, unfolding long elegant legs that made him think outrageous thoughts which he was sure must be almost audible, and he stood quickly beside her and turned to her mother.

'I'm sorry to have to cut and run like this, Mrs Blake.'

The woman smiled and Dan sensed that only an effort of will prevented her from patting his cheek. 'Don't be silly, Dan. It's happened in this family from the word go. We're used to it. You go and do what you have to do. We're just glad you were able to pop in at all.'

They made hasty farewells, and within minutes were on the road again. The snow had fortunately stopped, but the wind was bitter and icy and the snow was starting to pile up in drifts along the lanes. Twice they had to turn round and try a different route, and eventually they pulled up outside the Rudges' house. It was down a little lane on the opposite side of the village green to the practice and within easy walking distance of any supplies they might need to collect from the surgery, which Dan found a comforting thought.

Driving in the snow had never been his favourite thing. Being driven was infinitely worse, even if Holly was a good driver. Now she cut the engine, pulled out the keys and looked across at him. 'Did you want anything from the practice?'

'Have you got any salbutamol with you?'

She nodded. 'Yes—a little suspension and an inhaler. What about a drip?'

'I've got that, but hopefully she won't need it.'

'Let's go, then.'

Taking their bags, they tramped up the path to the front door and rang the bell.

Mr Rudge opened the door almost immediately, visibly relieved to see them. 'She's getting worse,' he said worriedly. 'We wondered whether to call an ambulance.'

'Let's look at her first,' Dan said calmly, and followed the man through to the sitting room where Becky was propped up against some cushions, a bowl of steaming water beside her, coughing and whooping and retching in turn until in the end she subsided against the cushions looking wan and tearful.

'Poor little love,' Dan said softly, and Holly hung back and let him examine her. He was brief. It didn't take a great deal of assessment to see the problems she was having, and she was clearly very dehydrated.

Dan shot a glance at the window, then looked at Holly.

'Long way to Norwich,' he murmured.

'Yes.'

'I've got a small-bore cannula and some saline in my bag. We could run some fluids into her, give her some salbutamol to help her clear her chest and just sit it out.'

'It might be safer,' Holly agreed. 'The roads are lethal. Perhaps in daylight it might be better if we can just keep her hydrated until the morning.'

Mrs Rudge hovered anxiously. 'Will she be all right?' she whispered.

Dan patted her hand comfortingly. 'Of course she will. She just needs a little more support than she's getting. We're going to set up a drip, give her some asthma-type drugs to help her breathe better and by the morning she'll probably be over the worst. Whatever, taking her out in this tonight would be madness. If it's necessary she can go to hospital tomorrow, but I'm hoping it won't be.'

They created as sterile an environment as possible to put the IV line in, and once it was in and the screaming had subsided Holly coaxed a spoonful of salbutamol suspension into Becky and sat back and crossed her fingers that it would stay down long enough to do some good.

It did, and after a few minutes her coughing eased. She didn't vomit again and as the drip ran in her skin slowly started to plump up over the next hour or so.

The Rudges made them tea and sandwiches, and they all sat around in the little sitting room, watching television, with one eye on Becky. After a while she went to sleep.

Dan pulled on his coat and boots and tramped back to the practice, let the dogs out for a run in the garden, fed them and then tramped back, armed with more saline and further supplies of salbutamol, both suspension and a nebuliser to supply a mist of the drug to be inhaled directly to the source of the problem—the lungs themselves.

Becky was still resting, her colour better and her skin plumping up nicely. They stayed a little longer until Dan was satisfied that she was sufficiently rehydrated, and then he gave the Rudges some more salbutamol suspension to give her over the next few hours, if necessary. He warned them about the dangers of giving too much, showed them how to work the nebuliser and when and told them to call if they were at all worried.

He took down the drip, taped over the cannula and left it in place in case they needed to put the drip up again in a hurry and finally they were back in the car and heading round the side of the village green towards the practice.

The wind had dropped and they were able to pick their way around the drifts, reaching the cottage just as the clock on the church tower struck two.

'Another early night,' Dan said with a sigh.

Holly chuckled wearily.

'All part of life's rich pattern. Isn't that why you became a doctor, Dan?'

He turned towards her, amazed that—as tired as he was—he could still appreciate the delicate symmetry of her face. 'Just at the moment, Holly, I can't remember why I became a doctor.'

'To save kids like Becky, of course,' she reminded him.

His smile was wry. He thought of his upbringing in the house on Regent's Park, of the clinic in Harley Street. 'Maybe,' he said softly. 'Maybe. . .'

CHAPTER FIVE

THE alarm woke Holly long before she was ready to be disturbed. The rest of the bright and bitter night had been mercifully quiet but even so she snuggled back under the covers and tried her best to ignore the alarm.

It was the light tap on her shoulder that penetrated the fog of sleep—that and Dan's softly gruff voice.

'Wake up, sleepyhead. Cup of tea for you. Surgery in half an hour.'

She rolled onto her back, pushed the quilt away from her face and cracked an eye open. He was standing by the bed, fully dressed in shirt, tie and trousers, and he looked as if he'd been up for ages. She struggled to a sitting position and took the tea, gratefully burying her nose in the steaming mug.

'Any news of Becky?'

'Yes, she's fine. I went over this morning and took out the cannula. She seems to have turned the corner of that particular crisis and the salbutamol seems to be effective in helping her breathe so, as long as she continues to improve, we can relax.'

'Good. Any patients here?'

'A couple. I've seen to them. Julia and Amy are on their way—Amy may be a little late as she's coming from Holt and the roads aren't all that clear yet, but there isn't anybody booked for the nurse early on so it won't matter. So long as Julia's here to get the phone we should manage.'

'Where does she come from?'

He waved in the general direction of the village green. 'Julia's Ted Simpkin's daughter from Church Farm—where Joel Stephens works. Great advantage of having local staff—they can get in come hell or high water.'

Holly, cradling her hot mug of tea, thought last night probably qualified as both. There had been a time when she'd wondered if they would get through without the Discovery and had regretted returning it to her father, but the four-wheel-drive Subaru had proved very efficient and hopefully the snow ploughs and gritters would be out today—before she had to make any house calls!

Conscious that it was her first proper day at work and that she would be meeting the other members of the practice team for the first time, she showered quickly and dressed with care, aiming for approachable professionalism without sacrificing her gender.

She might as well have worn a sack. Julia gave her a searching look and was not over-friendly, Amy—when she arrived—was equally noncommittal and the patients seemed torn between annoyance because they didn't have Dan to themselves and relief that their beloved Dr Elliott had some help at last!

Holly admired spotty tonsils and listened to gurgling chests and examined sprains and heard about Aunt Lena's bunions and thought longingly of the breakfast she'd forsaken so that she was able to make a good impression.

Then a fairly obese woman patient came in, eyed her assessingly and sniffed. 'You don't look very bright. Out living it up during New Year, were you? You look as if you haven't been to bed for days. Can't do that round here, you know. Decent folks go to bed at a respectable hour.'

Holly dragged out a professional smile. 'I'm afraid my revelling was done last night over a patient. If I look tired it's all happened in the course of duty.'

The woman, far from being appeased, sniffed again. 'No stamina, eh? Won't be a lot of use to our Dr Elliott if you can't take the odd call at night.'

Holly almost ground her teeth with impatience and kept the smile on with difficulty. 'I can assure you I have quite sufficient stamina. It's only my complexion that suffers. Bags under the eyes run in the family. Now, Mrs Peake, what can I do for you?'

'I've got heartburn,' she told Holly. 'I often have it, but it's been playing up more recently. I wondered if you could give me anything for it? Of course I expect you'll have to ask Dr Elliott before you can give me any drugs.'

Holly eyed her patiently. 'Mrs Peake, I'm a fully qualified GP. There's nothing Dr Elliott can treat that I can't. Now, you say it's been worse recently. How recently? Since you started eating richer food over the Christmas period?'

'Well—yes, I suppose so. That's it, of course. I suppose you're going to say it's my own fault—'

'Not at all.' Holly produced a genuine smile. 'We all overindulge at Christmas. You've probably had the odd bit to drink that you wouldn't normally have had as well.'

A tinge of colour ran up the woman's throat. 'I might have had the occasional glass of sherry.'

Holly bit the inside of her cheek to stop the smile. Occasional? She was sure now that the cause of Mrs

Peake's problem was oesophagitis caused by serious overindulgence on top of obesity, but she'd tackle one thing at a time. She checked quickly through the notes.

'Have you had any treatment in the past for this?'

'No—well, only antacids I've bought at the chemist. There's never been a need before.'

'Is it worse when you bend over or after a meal?'

Mrs Peake nodded slowly. 'It does tend to be—and I haven't been able to enjoy my Christmas cake the way I usually do. Do you think—? My mother had a hiatus hernia—is it possible I've inherited it?'

Holly nodded. 'The tendency can run in families. Whatever, the initial treatment is the same. I want to try you on a course of ranitidine. Now, it has a few occasional side-effects in a very small number of people. You might find you get a headache, or a slight skin rash or nausea. You'll possibly become constipated and you might feel a bit tired and lethargic, but anything like that and I'd like you to come back so I can review the treatment. I'd like to see you again anyway in ten days, but I doubt if you'll feel anything except the benefits. Hopefully, you'll be feeling much better within a couple of days.'

'Right.' The woman took the prescription from Holly's hand almost reluctantly. 'You say these side-effects are rare?'

'Very. You shouldn't worry. I only mentioned them just in case you had a headache, for instance. Even if you do it might be unrelated.' Holly was beginning to regret cautioning the woman. All drugs had some side-effects, and the side-effects of ranitidine weren't common and were never very severe. She had heard of one severe reaction, but that was through the medical

press and so isolated that it was entirely unlikely Mrs
Peake would suffer from it.

She sent her on her way, relieved that she was the
last patient in her surgery. She stood up and stretched,
left the room and went into the kitchen. Dan was in there
with Julia and Amy, and as she went in the conversation
stopped for a second.

Were they talking about her? Oh, damn, why did she
care? So his practice staff weren't friendly. So what?
He was hardly friendly, either. Perhaps that was what
they all saw in each other.

'Coffee?' Dan said, sliding back his chair. She sat
down at the table and nodded.

'Please—and I don't suppose there's any chance of
some breakfast?'

He glowered at her—at least she thought he did. As
ever, it was hard to tell. 'Haven't you had breakfast?'

She sighed. 'No, I haven't. There wasn't time. I
thought it would be better spent covering up the ravages
of last night, but I might as well not have bothered. Mrs
Peake just told me I wasn't suitable because I'd clearly
been revelling too much over New Year and decent folk
went to bed at a proper hour.'

Dan chuckled. 'Gloria Peake is a pillar of the community and would take it on herself to make sure you
were suitable. Did you tell her the truth?'

Holly raised an eyebrow. 'I tried. She then told me I
clearly didn't have enough stamina to help you and I'd
be no good if I couldn't manage the odd night call.'

He laughed. Damn him, he actually threw back his
head and laughed. Holly scowled at him and went and
put a slice of bread in the toaster. 'I didn't think it
was funny.'

'No, I'm sure. So, what was wrong with her?'

'Heartburn.'

He laughed again. 'She's a bit of a boozer on the quiet, our Gloria. I expect, with Christmas, she's been indulging herself more than somewhat. What did you give her?'

'Ranitidine.'

He nodded. 'That's fine.'

'I know it's fine!' Holly snapped.

'Hey!' Dan raised his hands in surrender. 'Did I hit a nerve?'

'She implied that I wasn't qualified to treat her without referral to you,' Holly told him crossly. 'I think she decided I was about twenty and wet behind the ears. Then I warned her about the side-effects and I think I've probably put the wind up her. She'll probably take the first pill and get a crippling headache or terminal constipation, and it'll be my fault!'

That set Dan off again, and as Holly turned she noticed Julia and Amy looking at him in amazement and exchanging significant smiles. Didn't he laugh usually? Probably not, or at least not recently. Was she responsible for that? A little glow wrapped round her heart and took away some of the chill that had settled there.

'Any calls for me to make, Julia?' she asked, returning to the table with her toast and coffee.

'Three, all fairly close to the village. The furthest is two miles. Here.' She slid some patient envelopes across the table to her. They had stick-on notes attached to them with brief symptoms. 'I'll write out directions so you don't get lost. The area can be a bit tricky.'

Holly glanced at the slips and the addresses and shook her head. 'No need. I know where all these places are.'

She bit into her toast, missing the look Julia gave her.
'If you're sure—' she began.

'I am. Dan, any news of Jeremiah Sproat?'

'No. Want to ring?'

'I think I will. If I'm over that way, seeing this patient, I may as well go the extra mile and check him.' She found the number in the telephone directory, dialled it and spoke to Mrs Sproat then hung up.

'Well?'

'Much the same, she said. I'll pop in. How's the drifting this morning?'

'No worse than it was when we left Becky's. The wind's dropped. If you're going over there shall I take the call in the village and go and check Becky again while I'm at it?'

She glared at him. 'No, you shan't. That's not the deal. I do the calls, you take the emergency surgeries. And, anyway, you shouldn't be out in the cold with that chest. Are you still taking the antibiotics?'

Julia and Amy looked from Dan to her and back again.

'Antibiotics?' they chorused.

'Mmm, he's had bronchitis—didn't he tell you? He should have been in bed for the past couple of days, but would he go?' She snorted expressively. 'That's men for you. Always got to struggle on until they drop— either that or they're the worst babies in the world.'

'Ego,' Julia said. It was the first time she'd said anything that could have been a friendly, chatty overture, and Holly nearly choked on her toast. Surely they weren't unbending?

No. Amy gathered up her professional demeanour and gave Holly a stiff look. 'He's had no choice but to struggle on. It's been very difficult.'

Holly smiled pacifyingly. 'I know, but I'm here now. He can keel over and relax.'

She pushed back her chair, picked up the patient envelopes Julia had given her and reached for her coat. 'Hi-ho, hi-ho,' she said with a smile. 'See you all later. I'll expect a better lunch, Dan.'

He muttered something rude under his breath and she chuckled, patted the dogs in passing and went out into the cold but sunny day.

It was glorious now, quite different to yesterday evening, she thought, and turned her face up to the sun. No warmth to speak of, but a glorious light. She climbed into the car, started the engine and ran it for a moment to heat the windscreen, then pulled out carefully and headed off to her first call.

In the kitchen Dan stood up and went through to his surgery, and Julia and Amy exchanged glances.

'I wonder how long she'll last out here in the middle of nowhere?'

Julia shook her head. 'Not long. Too remote, isn't it? I'd leave if it wasn't for Peter, but we can't take the farm with us. Anyway, it's my home.'

'How's the cottage coming on?'

She pulled a face. 'Slowly. I don't know if it'll be ready for the wedding. Weather's hardly on our side, is it?'

Amy stood up. 'It'll be a shame if she does go. I haven't seen Dan laugh for nearly two years.'

'No.'

'She will go, though. They always do.'

'Mmm. Oh, well, while she's here it'll give the gossips something to do, them living together.'

'They have to.'

'I know—but it would be easier to explain if she was a man or ancient or ugly.' Julia laughed. 'Even then, some of this lot would find something in it.'

'Maybe there is—or will be. She's pretty.'

Julia murmured agreement. 'Shame it can't last.'

Dan, standing in his hallway outside the kitchen, had to agree with them. Inevitably she would go—and it was a shame. She was more than pretty, she was well and truly under his skin already.

Turning quietly, he went back into his room, shut the door and leant against it with a sigh. If she stayed she'd tie him in knots, and if she went he realised he'd miss her, even after less than two days. He was damned either way.

The rest of the day was uneventful. Holly did her calls, checked Jeremiah Sproat and found him much the same. At least he didn't seem to be any worse and the pall of smoke was gone from the room, but they might simply have opened the window before she came.

Becky was looking much brighter, although her parents looked exhausted. At least the child was still at home, and Holly was sure they would have been much more worried and exhausted had they made the trip to Norwich to the hospital the night before.

Her later surgery was unremarkable, and during the afternoon she heard Mrs Hodges vacuuming the carpets upstairs in her rooms and then pottering in the kitchen. Delicious smells started to waft through the door and Holly, who had found the instant soup and toast for lunch woefully inadequate, wondered if she would get through her surgery without fainting with anticipation.

As she finished up her last patient and went through

to the kitchen, she found Dan in there, poking about in a big pot on the stove.

'What is it?' she asked.

'Dunno. Chicken something beginning with M.'

'Marengo?'

'That's it.'

'Wow.' Holly leant over and sniffed the glorious rich casserole. 'I could eat it all.'

'Feel free, it's done. There are some jacket potatoes in the oven, and peas ready to cook on the top. Shall I put them on?'

'Please. Mind if I just go and change into something more casual?'

He shook his head. 'Be my guest. You've got five minutes.'

Holly laughed. 'I won't be that long. I'm too hungry.'

She ran up the stairs, changed into her jeans and an old sweatshirt—while she noted with pleasure that the room was clean and tidy, the bed which she had leapt out of neatly made, the bathroom spotless—and then ran downstairs again.

'Three.'

'What?'

'Three minutes. You've been three minutes. Here, drink this.'

Dan handed her a glass of white wine, and with a sigh she shook her head. 'I might get a call. I need to be sober.'

He smiled. 'It's alcohol-free.'

'In which case—' She grinned and relieved him of it. 'Mmm, lovely. Are the peas done?'

Dan chuckled. 'Are you hungry, by any chance?'

She laughed. 'Just a bit.'

He dished up while she laid the table, and within moments she was tucking in.

'I love Mrs Hodges,' she said round a mouthful.

'So do I,' Dan agreed. 'If it wasn't out of the question I'd marry her.'

'How old is she?'

'Fifty-five.'

'That's not impossible.'

Dan gave a wry grin. 'Her husband would think it was.'

'Ah. Forgot about him. You could always bump him off.'

'I could. She might go into a decline, though, and forget how to cook.'

Holly shuddered. 'Pass on that, then. Keep him fit.'

'I intend to!'

They exchanged a smile, and Holly promptly forgot about her food and how hungry she was. She forgot about everything except the firm, sculpted lips of the man sitting opposite her and how good they had felt against hers. She wanted to reach out and pull off those hateful glasses and look into his wonderful granite-blue eyes and thread her fingers through his hair and pull his head down until his mouth met hers and then—

The phone rang, snatching her from her fantasy just before she disgraced herself by drooling over him.

Dan passed her the phone. 'Call for you. I think it's one of the Rottweilers.'

She took the receiver, turned away from him and lifted it to her ear. 'Hello?'

'Holly? It's Michael.'

'Hi. How is everything?'

'Fine. Are you all right?'

'Yes, of course I am.'

'I tried to ring last night—all I got was the answerphone.'

Holly sighed. 'Did you leave a message?'

'No. It's a bit difficult to leave a message on a man's answerphone, warning your sister off him.'

She sighed again. 'Why would you want to do that, Michael?'

'He's too old for you—not just in age, but everything. He's been around the block a few times, Holly, got a reputation. His wife's a bitch, he's from an incredibly wealthy background, his parents are divorced, his father's got a roving eye, he's divorced—Holly, the guy's a loser emotionally. And he's got the hots for you.'

'Michael, don't be vulgar,' she reprimanded him, thinking as she did so that the expression summed up her fantasy pretty accurately.

'Holly, it's true. We're all worried sick—all except Mum. She says—well, never mind what she says.'

'What does she say, Michael?'

He mumbled for a moment, then at her persistence he confessed, 'She says it's time someone woke you up to the fact that you're a woman, and Dan Elliott might be just man enough to do it.'

Well, hooray for Mother, Holly thought fondly. Holly had just reached the same conclusion herself.

She wound her brother up as well as she could, without revealing the content of her conversation to Dan, but as she hung up the phone and turned back to Dan she could see from his face that he wasn't fooled.

'More growling and snapping?'

She grinned. 'He loves me.'

Dan sighed and shook his head. 'You're safe, Holly. I'm not going to touch you.'

'Shame,' she said softly.

Not softly enough. His head snapped up and he looked straight at her—at least, she thought he did. For once she was glad of the glasses.

She looked down at her meal. Suddenly she'd lost interest. There were other things—more important things—on her mind. Like that kiss she'd been thinking about when the phone rang—

'Holly, forget it. I'm not on the market.'

Her head came up again. 'Who said I wanted to buy?'

'Just sampling the goods?' he said softly. 'No, Holly. I don't want to play games like that.'

'Then what do you want?'

'A professional colleague.'

'Is that why you kissed me?'

There was a palpable silence, then Dan pushed back his chair and stood up, busying himself at the sink. 'That was a mistake,' he muttered.

'Was it?'

She pushed back her own chair and went over to him. 'Was it?'

For a moment he stood there with his back to her then, with a muttered curse, he pushed her aside, grabbed his coat and boots, whistled for the dogs and left, banging the front door behind him.

Holly sat down again and finished her casserole, cleared the table, loaded the dishwasher, switched it on and made herself a cup of tea. She was just sitting down to drink it when the phone rang again.

It was Mr Peake, Gloria Peake's husband, and he sounded frantic. 'Dr Elliott, please, now.'

'I'm sorry, he's out. Can I help you? I'm his locum—I saw your wife this morning, Mr Peake.'

'Are you the stupid woman who gave her these pills?'

Suddenly Holly had a bad, bad feeling. 'I did prescribe a drug for her, yes,' she replied. 'Why, does there seem to be a problem?'

'Her tongue,' he said frantically. 'It's swollen up so much she can't shut her mouth. She looks terrible.'

'How many of the pills has she taken?'

'Just one.'

'I'm coming now. Tell her to sit up and lean forwards against something firm, and I'll be with you in a couple of minutes. Give me directions.'

She scribbled them down and just as she was pulling on her coat, Dan came back in with the dogs.

'Look, Holly, I'm sorry,' he began.

She grabbed his arm. 'No time for that. Gloria Peake's had an allergic reaction to the ranitidine—at least I suppose it is. Her tongue's swollen.'

'Her tongue? My God, I've only ever read about that once.'

'Me, too. Probably the same article. We need adrenaline and corticosteroids—probably a drip, too.'

'I'll get everything. She'll have to go to Norwich. We can call an ambulance once we see her. I'll get the things to do a trachy.'

'Oh, God.' Holly closed her eyes and leant against the wall. What if the woman died? Would it be her fault? Seconds later she had pulled herself together and was out in the car with the engine running while she waited for Dan.

He wasn't long. As he threw himself into the car he yelled, 'Go.' She needed no further encouragement.

Only the condition of the roads made her go slowly, and she was hideously conscious of Mrs Peake's dangerous condition and the necessity for speed.

After what seemed like an age they pulled up outside a big red-brick and flint house on the edge of the village. Almost before the car was parked Dan was thrusting the door open and heading up the path.

Holly followed only slightly more slowly, arriving at the door just as it was thrown open against its hinges.

'Dr Elliott—come in, for God's sake, man. She's in the kitchen.'

They hurried through and found Mrs Peake slumped over the table, her tongue hugely swollen and protruding and her breath rasping.

'Mrs Peake?' Dan crouched beside her, taking her hand and talking to her reassuringly as he assessed her. Holly, too, was assessing the situation and she didn't like it one bit.

'Trachy?' she murmured.

'Yes. Let's get some adrenaline and steroids into her fast, then we'll do it. Right, Mrs Peake, we're going to give you something to take down the reaction a bit. You'll just feel a little scratch on your hand.'

'Scratch coming now,' Holly told her, but the hand was pulled away and the woman's eyes, already wide with fear, widened still further as she flapped her hands at Holly.

'I think she wants you to do it, Dr Elliott,' Holly said quietly, and handed him the syringe. He found the vein, slipped the needle home and slowly delivered the drugs, then pulled the needle out.

'We need a cannula in there, too, and a saline drip. She's a bit shocked.'

'What about the airway?'

'We'll give the adrenaline a minute or two to see if it works. She's coping at the moment. I'll phone for an ambulance.'

The adrenaline, however, couldn't seem to keep pace with the effects of the drug and as he put the phone down Dan turned to Holly. 'We'll have to do it now.'

She nodded and while he explained what they were going to do she found the sterile packs Dan had brought and laid them out on the worktop. The kitchen was mercifully spotless, and the table a big refectory-style table long enough to take Mrs Peake lying down.

Dan infiltrated the front of Mrs Peake's throat with local anaesthetic and then while it took effect they scrubbed as well as they could at the sink, pulled on gloves and then helped the frantic woman onto the table. She was still flapping Holly away, but as she lay down and her tongue slid to the back of her throat she ceased to worry about her.

Her husband hovered in the way, holding her hand and gazing in horror at the scalpel Dan held poised in his hand.

'Sit down, Mr Peake,' Dan told him firmly, and then sliced down into the windpipe. He made a gap just big enough to take a tracheotomy tube, inserted the tube and sighed audibly as Mrs Peake took a huge, gasping breath and relaxed. He taped the tube in place, tugged off his gloves and stroked her forehead.

'Better?'

She nodded slightly and Holly went over to the sink to remove her gloves and wash her hands, aware as she did so of her shaking legs which would hardly carry her. The patient was seriously ill—might even have died—and all because she had prescribed a drug to which the woman was allergic.

'You weren't to know,' Dan said softly in her ear. 'I would have given her exactly the same drug. It's not your fault.'

'I feel as if it is,' she began, but he made a silent shh-ing gesture with his lips as Mr Peake came over to them.

'Will she be all right now?' he asked. 'What about her tongue?'

Dan turned and laid a hand on his shoulder. 'She'll be fine, Mr Peake. She needs to go to hospital, of course, and over the next few hours her tongue will reduce to its normal size and she'll be able to breathe again without the tube.'

'It was the drug, wasn't it?'

Dan nodded. 'It looks like it. It's an extremely rare complication of the treatment. I've never come across it in eight years of general practice and I've never heard of anyone else who has, except in a medical journal. I can only say I'm sorry she reacted this way.'

'It's a dangerous drug—she was going on about all the side-effects before she took it.'

'The side-effects are usually very minor and unremarkable—'

'Unremarkable! Look at her, man! She's at death's door!'

'Not really,' Dan said soothingly. 'And it's a very useful and helpful drug. I have several patients on it— over the years I've prescribed it probably hundreds of times without any ill-effect at all. Your wife was just very unfortunate.'

Mr Peake levelled a finger at Dan and then at Holly.

'You'll hear more about this—especially you, young woman. Are you sure you're properly qualified?'

'Quite sure,' she said, more firmly than she felt. Just then she didn't feel qualified to read a thermometer, but she wasn't telling him that.

They saw the flashing lights of the ambulance bouncing off the snow, and Holly sighed with relief and went to the door to let them in. Minutes later their patient was loaded and away and they were back at the cottage.

Holly was still shaking, and Dan pushed her into a chair and made them a cup of tea, then slid hers across the table to her. 'Here. Drink this.'

She sipped it and pulled a face. 'It's sweet.'

'Mmm. You look shocked.'

'Not that shocked,' she denied, grimacing at the mug. 'Drink it.'

She did, finding as she did so that it didn't taste that bad after all. She set the mug down and looked at Dan across the table. 'Do you think they'll sue?'

He shrugged. 'They might try. It wouldn't hurt to contact the Medical Defence Union on Monday and put them in the picture, but I honestly don't think they've got a case. There's no way you could have anticipated that reaction—it's a commonly prescribed drug and it's something that could have happened to anybody.'

She lifted miserable eyes to his face. 'Dan?'

'Mmm?'

'I need a hug.'

He hesitated for a moment, then with a sigh he pushed himself to his feet, came round the table and caught her as she threw herself into his arms. 'I thought she was going to die,' she mumbled against his chest, 'when I saw her tongue all swollen up like that, I was sure she was going to die and it would be my fault—'

'Rubbish. Like I said, it could have happened to any-one.' His hand cupped the back of her head, soothing her with gentle strokes. It must be wonderful to be a dog, she thought hazily, and as she tipped her head back to say that to him he turned towards her and their mouths brushed accidentally.

That was all it took. With a despairing groan Dan's mouth settled over hers and her fantasy took flight. Her eyes fluttered shut, her lips parted and Dan took instant advantage. His tongue meshed with hers, running over the edge of her teeth—searching out the dark velvety secrets of her mouth—driving her wild.

She slid her hands up and threaded her fingers through his hair, sifting the soft, heavy strands like silk. Against her breasts she could feel the solid thud of his heart, and the beat of her own drowned out all reason. She leaned against him with a soft moan, and he gathered her up against his hard, lean body and plundered her mouth as if he would die without her.

Then, without warning, he pulled away and stood just inches from her, his chest heaving and a muscle working in his jaw.

'What is it about you?' he muttered almost savagely. 'Why is it that one taste just isn't enough?'

She didn't know. All she knew was that she felt the same—the only difference was that she was prepared to accept it and Dan wasn't.

Not by a country mile.

CHAPTER SIX

HOLLY spent that first weekend at Dan's torn between her natural instinct to pursue this thing that was happening between them and the more sensible option of running like crazy.

Running like crazy won in the end, but only because she was too busy to have time to plan an adequate strategy for her pursuit of Dan. She was also too worried about Mrs Peake and her swollen tongue to be able to concentrate on something as complex as rescuing Dan from himself.

So she waited, and she worked all weekend off and on because the snow meant that everybody would rather the doctor came to them. Surprise, surprise, she thought wryly, and remembered that Dan had been ill with bronchitis and was still coughing and it would do him good to have a bit of a rest.

The nights, at least, were fairly quiet, for which she was profoundly grateful. The snow refused to thaw, and although no more fell it was a major hazard on the roads.

The kids enjoyed it, though. She was driving back from a call on Sunday afternoon and saw them out on the hill behind the village, tobogganing down a slope in plastic feed sacks. There was a lot of giggling and yelling going on, the boys egging each other on and having races. Holly smiled to herself, remembering her own childhood days spent tobogganing with her brothers.

She turned onto the drive in front of the cottage and cut the engine. As she climbed out of the car she saw Dan tramping towards her across the green, the dogs bouncing round his heels. She went inside so that she could stand at the window and watch him, unobserved. It was a small enough reward for taking all the patients. A little treat for herself—and what a treat.

He looked wonderful, she thought, his body endowed with that fluid masculine grace of the natural athlete, still clearly visible despite his injuries. He moved well considering the severe fracture his leg had suffered. He must have worked hard at his physio. He still had the slightest trace of a limp—more a favouring of the damaged leg—and as she watched he paused and rubbed his thigh absently, his eyes trained on the hill behind the village and the tobogganing children.

Without warning he changed. She saw the sudden alertness, the change in posture from relaxation to immediate readiness, and as he started to sprint towards the hill she realised there must have been an accident.

She didn't hesitate. Her bag was in her car, she still had her coat and boots on and she was out there, heading towards the hill, within seconds.

She intercepted Dan as he reached the road and flung open the door. 'What's happened?' she yelled, climbing out.

'I don't know. One of the boys—they're tobogganing.'

'I know. Jump in—we'll drive round.'

He was in the car, with the dogs piled into the back, almost before the words were out of her mouth and she headed up behind the cottages to the track that led to the field where the children were. As they bumped along the track it was obvious from the cessation of activity that something fairly major had happened. She pulled up, and they jumped out and ran up the hill towards the cluster of quiet children.

They could hear someone sobbing and as they arrived at the group one of the children turned and recognised Dan, and the look of relief on his face was almost comical. 'It's all right, Dave, Dr Elliott's here.'

The crowd parted, as if by magic, to reveal a young lad sprawled on his side in the snow, bent over and clutching something—his leg—inside a torn and bloodied plastic sack.

Dan crouched down beside him. 'What have you done, David? What's happened?'

'Something sharp,' the boy sobbed. 'My leg—'

There was a bright red stain on the snow and as Dan pulled the sack away the stain spread, vivid against the virgin white.

The boy was drenched in blood, and she could see it welling from the back of his thigh and flooding the ripped jeans. There was no need to make a closer examination there and then. The obvious and most important thing was to move him to somewhere warm, clean and dry and get that cut exposed and treated. First they had to stop the bleeding.

Dan ripped off his scarf, folded it into a tight wad and then held his hand out to Holly. Mourning the loss of her new Christmas present, she handed Dan the cream lambswool scarf her older brother had given her and watched as he used it to bind his wadded scarf in place against the boy's thigh to act as a pressure pad over the wound.

'Someone go and find his parents and get them to

meet us at the surgery, please,' Dan said to the crowd as he tightened the scarf and checked that the pressure pad was working. Satisfied, he straightened up. 'Right, let's move him.' There were plenty of strong lads about, and they formed a chair and carried him down to the car where Dan installed him on the back seat, before getting in the front next to Holly.

'Right, go!' he said, but she already was, reversing carefully out onto the road and then making the short journey to the practice. Together they carried David into the surgery and went straight into the treatment room which Dan used for minor surgical techniques. While Holly found a pair of scissors and cut up the back of David's jeans to expose the wound Dan was scrubbing and donning a gown.

'Are you going to stitch it?' Holly asked quietly, surprised that he wasn't just going to admit the boy.

'I don't know. If he's nicked an artery I won't, but if it's just a nasty gash we could treat him here—I'd like to see the damage before I decide.'

Holly untied the pressure pad, sparing not a glance for her ruined scarf, and peeled away the jeans. The gash was jagged and about six inches long, but the blood seemed to have slowed to a steady seep.

Dan frowned at it. 'I'd like to know how deep it is, and I'd dearly love to know what he cut it on.'

He bent over so his head was near the boy's, and put his hand on his shoulder. 'David, have you any idea what it might have been?'

He nodded. 'There's an old plough there near the side—I expect it was that. Mostly we were sliding down the middle of the field, but it's a bit steeper there near the edge.' His voice wobbled. 'I thought it would make it more exciting.'

'Well, it certainly did that,' Dan said drily. 'You've got a nasty cut and I'd like to take a closer look at it, but it might hurt. I want you to be brave for me, OK?'

He nodded, and Holly moved up to his head and comforted him as Dan eased the sides of the gash open and dabbed with a saline-soaked swab to clear away the blood.

'*Ow!*' he yelled and, grabbing Holly's hand, he clung onto it like a lifeline.

'Seems quite clean,' Dan murmured from further down the couch. 'We'll need to irrigate it to be certain, and I want to know exactly what it was before I stitch him up, but there's no arterial damage of any significance and it's not as deep as I'd feared.'

'He'll need a tetanus booster, won't he?'

'I'm not sure. David, how old are you?'

'Thirteen,' the lad replied tearfully.

'In which case, yes. They have one routinely at fourteen so he's about due. Right, Holly, if you could help me get his jeans off and clean him up, ready for a closer look, we should be able to make a start as soon as his parents arrive.'

In fact, although it was a messy tear, once they infiltrated it with local anaesthetic and could study it without hurting him they found that it looked a lot worse than it actually was. Whatever had caused it had missed the many vital structures it could so easily have damaged had it been a little deeper.

They were told that, yes, it had been the edge of an old plough, abandoned by the side of the field, on which he had caught his leg. As the field was David's father's there was the issue of his guilt to be dealt with as well, but they left David's mother to sort that one out.

It took a long time, nearly an hour, to clean the wound and check it to Dan's satisfaction and stitch it. Fortunately the damage was along the line of the muscle and not across it, which meant it would heal much quicker and with much less likelihood of future problems.

By the time David and his parents left the surgery it was six o'clock in the evening and Holly was predictably starving. Dan pulled a couple of plated-up dinners out of the freezer and thawed them in the microwave, and they sat down at the kitchen table and ate them, still talking about David and his lucky escape.

'Do you think he'll have much of a scar?' Holly asked.

Dan shrugged. 'I did my best. Hopefully not.'

'Not that it would matter on the back of his leg,' Holly said blithely, taking another mouthful of her hastily thawed meal.

'Scars matter wherever they are.'

She looked up sharply at Dan's softly voiced comment, and found his mouth was drawn into a tight line. Oh, dear. Yet again she'd blundered in where angels would have had more sense.

She wondered what his eyes were saying but, of course, as usual it was impossible to tell.

'I wish you'd take them off,' she blurted out, without thinking.

He gave a short sigh and shot his chair back as he stood abruptly. 'You don't learn, do you?'

'Learn what? To keep out, to leave your walls alone and let you isolate yourself behind them without any human contact? No, I don't.'

'Maybe I don't want human contact, Holly. Maybe this is nothing to do with my accident. Did you ever stop to think of that?'

She searched his face—what she could see of it. His mouth was set in a bleak line and she knew, without seeing them, that his eyes would be sad and empty. 'Oh, Dan,' she murmured. 'I'm sorry.'

'For what? Your phenomenal lack of tact?'

She flinched from the savagely accurate criticism. 'No,' she said wistfully. 'For whatever's made you so sad and lonely and bitter and afraid to love.'

He gave a harsh bark of laughter. 'Who on earth is talking about love? One minute we're discussing David's leg, the next minute you're talking about love. You're either unbelievably stupid or you've got an ego the size of a house. Possibly both.' The door banged behind him, leaving her alone in the kitchen with the dogs. They whined and looked beseechingly at her, lost without their master.

She stood up with a sigh and scraped her food into the dogs' dishes. Suddenly her appetite was gone, and they seemed to appreciate the meal more than her. Then she went upstairs to her room, closed the door firmly but quietly behind her and sat down.

So he didn't want her offer of friendship—or any other more personal or intimate offer she might have been about to make. Who could tell what she'd been about to say? Certainly not her.

'All the tact of a fox in a henhouse,' she said crossly, hurling a cushion across the room. It hit the wall opposite and fell to the floor, harmlessly defusing her anger and frustration.

She was no good to him at all. Between giving him

a hard time about his glasses and trying to kill off his patients, she was doing precious little to make his life easier, she thought.

Feeling guilty and still too worried about Mrs Peake to concentrate on the television, she fetched the book from her bedside table where it had laid unopened since her arrival, and tried to lose herself in it. It was a good book, one she'd enjoyed the beginning of and had been looking forward to finishing, but once again she was thwarted.

The phone rang—Jeremiah Sproat had taken a turn for the worse, and could she go over? She could. She bundled up in her warm clothes, left a note for Dan in the kitchen, rather than knocking on his door, and drove the four miles to the farm.

Snow had drifted a little more onto the drive but the Subaru managed with difficulty and a lot of sliding and skidding about, and when she arrived and climbed out Mrs Sproat hurried her into the kitchen and closed the door, shutting out the north-easterly that blasted straight off the sea and across the heath.

'How is he?' Holly asked without preamble.

'Worse, much worse. Coughing dreadfully badly and his colour's gone terrible. His lips were all blue at one time, and he couldn't seem to catch his breath at all.'

Holly didn't like the sound of it in the slightest. She went into the bedroom and found the old man lying listlessly against a pile of pillows. His temperature was down a little but his condition was far worse, and Holly wondered if there was a more sinister underlying cause to his illness.

She listened to his chest again and found that sounds in one part of it were completely absent now, as if the air was quite obstructed from that section of lung. She had brought a portable oxygen cylinder with her from the surgery, and she set it up and put a mask over his face.

Within minutes his breathing eased and his colour improved, but both changes were marginal and insufficient.

'Mrs Sproat, I'm sorry, he's going to have to go to hospital,' Holly said quietly to the man's daughter-in-law.

'He's got lung cancer, hasn't he?'

She met the woman's candid and accepting eyes, and nodded. 'I believe so. We can't be sure without tests and some pictures of his lungs, but I'm pretty certain there's something very wrong there.'

Mrs Sproat nodded. 'I've got a case packed—thought it looked like a hospital job.'

'I'll use your phone to call an ambulance, if I may?'

'Of course, dear. You go and do that, and I'll tell the old boy where he's going. The phone's in the office—you know where that is, don't you?'

She nodded and, going out, she went down the corridor to the farm office and tapped on the door. Jeremiah's son, John, was sitting in there staring at the wall, a glass of whisky in his hand.

He spared her a glance, then his eyes fixed on the wall again. 'He's dying, isn't he?'

Holly perched on the desk near him. 'I'm afraid he may well be. I'd like to call an ambulance to take him to hospital.'

'He'll hate that. Can't he stay here?'

Holly chewed her lip. 'He won't get the treatment he needs here.'

'Will it make any difference in the end?'

She had to admit that, no, it probably wouldn't make any difference at all. Even so, she was unhappy about allowing him to stay. There was always the chance she was wrong. 'I'd be happier if he was in hospital—'

'How about him, Dr Blake? How will he feel, dying away from his home? He's lived here in this house his whole hundred years, apart from going away towards the end of the First World War. The Great War, he calls it. He was in the trenches—lucky to come home. This here's *his* herd really.' He jabbed a thumb at the wall, and Holly noticed for the first time the prize certificates and rosettes and photographs taken at various county and national shows over the years.

Jeremiah was in most of them, a wizened little grape of a man with twinkling eyes and the indomitable spirit of a true fighter. It seemed a shame for such a man to be forced to undergo a whole battery of tests that in the end would prove nothing except what they already knew.

Jeremiah wasn't going to get his telegram because he wasn't going to make it to his birthday.

'Mind if I call Dr Elliott? I'd like to talk to him before I make a decision. He's his patient, really, I'm only the locum.' With Mr Peake's threats still ringing in her ears, Holly wasn't about to trust her professional judgement further than she could throw it.

Dan answered on the second ring, and she quickly filled him in. 'Would you like to see him yourself?'

'Do you want me to?'

'Please,' she said quietly. 'I'll come and get you.'

It took half an hour to get back to Wiventhorpe, and another half hour to return to the farm. As they drove in the Sproats met them at the door, and she knew it was all over.

'He just slipped away,' Mrs Sproat told them. 'I said he'd have to go to hospital, and he said the only way he was going out of that door was in a box, and the next thing he just seemed to fade in front of me. It was ever so peaceful, really. . .'

Her eyes welled, and she turned her head into her husband's shoulder and he gave her an awkward little hug and a pat. Uncomfortable with emotion, they were nevertheless both very shocked and saddened, and Dan and Holly stayed with them and shared a cup of tea while they waited for the ambulance. Dan assured them they had done everything necessary and possible for him, and then the ambulance came and Old Jeremiah was taken away. Then Holly drove Dan back to the cottage along the frozen, snow-covered lanes. It was icy and bitterly cold, and she was concentrating on driving with part of her mind, the other part lingering still with the old man. Maybe if she'd admitted him—

'Well, he got what he wanted,' Dan said, his quiet voice interrupting Holly's melancholy train of thought.

'Hmm?'

'Jeremiah. He left the house as he wanted—in a box, so to speak—after ending his days in his home surrounded by his family. He would have hated anything else.'

'I suppose so.'

'Holly, you know it's true.'

She sighed, then an icy stretch of road demanded her attention and she forgot about Jeremiah until they arrived back at the cottage.

They went into the kitchen to a rapturous greeting

from the dogs, and as they hung up their coats and kicked off their boots Dan turned to Holly. 'Drink?' he asked her, as if he knew she didn't want to be alone.

'Thanks.'

They made coffee, and he led her into the sitting room and settled her in front of the fire, and they talked for hours about old Jeremiah and life and death and Mrs Peake and making professional decisions that turned out to be the wrong ones and others that turned out to be right.

'He would have died on the way to hospital,' Dan said for the umpteenth time. 'It was much the best way as it was. Quiet, peaceful, dignified, with his family round him—what more could a man ask for?'

'He never got his telegram,' Holly said sadly, and then the tears splashed over and she apologised and set her cup down and slopped her coffee, and then—before she could do anything else stupid—she was in Dan's arms, and he was holding her and rocking her and murmuring all the right sorts of things, and after a while she settled down and just enjoyed being in his arms.

'He had a good life,' Dan told her.

'I saw the pictures of the bulls and the heifers at the shows.'

'His pride and joy, that herd.'

'Dan, if I'd admitted him on Thursday do you think he'd still be alive now?'

Dan sighed softly and stroked her hair. 'I don't know, Holly. I just know he'd have been miserable. He died where it was right for him to be. He couldn't get out and about round the farm any more, and without his beloved cows he was miserable. The BSE crisis nearly killed him. They lost a lot of their prize herd to the cull, and the stuffing seemed to go out of him after that. No, I think you did the right thing on Thursday, and I think you did the right thing tonight. You can't save everyone, Holly. He was almost a hundred.'

'I know.' She snuggled closer. 'It would just have been nice if he'd made it to his birthday,' she said with a sigh. 'I remember him from when I was a child. It seems really odd that he's gone. I must ring and tell my father—he'll want to go to the funeral. I'd like to, as well, if you can spare me. I don't know when it will be.'

'Of course I can spare you,' he murmured. His voice was very close, and she tipped her head back and smiled at him.

'Thanks, Dan,' she whispered, and then as naturally as day follows night, she lifted her lips to his.

It was a gentle kiss, undemanding, almost platonic at first, but then it deepened and warmed, still gentle but definitely a very sensuous caress. Then he lifted his head and tucked her closer so that his chin rested on her head and her ear was against his heart, and after a moment she heard a deep sigh echo through his chest.

'I didn't mean to do that,' he murmured, and she could hear the gentle regret in his voice.

'Why not?'

'Because it's crazy. It isn't going to lead anywhere, Holly.'

She lifted her head. 'Did I say it should? Or that I wanted it to?'

Gently, carefully, he put her from him and stood up. 'All women want more than they admit. There's always a hidden agenda.'

Holly studied him as he threw more logs into the wood-burner, then went to the window and lifted the curtain aside, staring out into the freezing night.

'What was your wife's?'

He dropped the curtain and turned back. 'What?'

'Your wife's hidden agenda. I just wondered what it was.'

Even with the glasses on she could see his face harden and grow cold, as cold as the night outside. 'I don't talk about my ex-wife,' he said tightly.

Holly refused to give up. 'She must have hurt you very much to make you so angry.'

He glared at her. 'It's none of your damn business, Holly. Leave me alone. I don't want to talk about her, I don't want to have a personal relationship with you, I don't want to kiss you again—'

'Liar,' she interrupted softly.

He froze, and with a muttered curse he flung open the door of his room.

'Goodnight, Dr Blake,' he said, and his voice cut her like a sliver of ice. She stood up, uncurling her legs and straightening slowly.

'Goodnight, Dan. Sweet dreams.'

She walked past him, conscious of the animosity flowing off him in waves. The door clicked shut behind her with rigidly controlled violence, and then there was a thump and a thud, as if he had punched his fist into something soft and hurled it across the room. A cushion? Not the cat, she hoped!

She smiled slightly. So she ruffled him. Good. It was only fair—he ruffled her well and truly. As she made herself a cup of tea and went up to her room she wondered what his wife had done to make him so bitter and twisted about women—or relationships with women, at least. He seemed to be able to cope well enough with his women patients, from the little she'd seen of him.

All she knew was that his wife—ex-wife, she corrected herself—had spent most of her time in London, and that he had apparently been around the block a few times, in her brother's vulgar parlance. He also, according to Michael, had the hots for her.

If so he was hurling cold water on those hots as hard as he could because apart from the very occasional lapse he was managing to keep his distance disappointingly well.

So, she thought, mulling over Michael's words again, he came from a wealthy but broken home. Was that significant? Dad had a roving eye—an inherited trait? Perhaps his wife had left him because he wasn't faithful—or perhaps because of his parents' failure he had had unrealistic expectations. She couldn't even begin to guess, and it was very obvious that Dan had absolutely no intention of discussing it with her in a cosy little chat over coffee one day.

'Oh, damn,' she said with a sigh, draining the last mouthful of her tea and setting the cup down. The television was awful so she tuned the radio to an easy listening station and curled up with her book. The phone was mercifully silent—so silent that she thought it was probably broken—but then she had a call from someone who just needed telephone advice and so she knew the thing was working, she just wasn't in demand.

They'd probably heard about Mrs Peake, she thought, and on the spur of the moment she rang the hospital in Norwich and was told that Mrs Peake was recovering well. Her tongue had gone down now, she was breathing without the tracheotomy tube and would probably be sent home on Tuesday or Wednesday.

And then, Holly thought, it'll really hit the fan. Oh, well.

She checked her watch. Eleven-thirty, but she really ought to ring her father and tell him about Jeremiah Sproat.

'Oh, dear, what a shame,' Phillip Blake said heavily as she passed on the news. 'He was one the last of the old farmers—knew the name of every beast and could spout you chapter and verse of its lineage. He was a good stockman, too. He had good instincts. I shall miss him. When will the funeral be?'

'I don't know. I'll let you know. I'm going.'

'I'll see you there. I'll get someone to cover my surgery if necessary. By the way, this chap Elliott—he is behaving properly, I take it?'

Holly sighed. 'Unfortunately, yes.'

'What?'

'I said of course he is, yes.'

'Hmm. I thought you said unfortunately.'

Holly crossed her fingers. 'Dad, why would I say that?'

'I can't imagine,' was the dry retort. 'Well, take care of yourself, sweetheart, and remember we're only just round the corner if you need us.'

'Thanks. Love to Mum.'

She hung up, then checked her watch. Ten to twelve. She didn't feel sleepy, but she might well have to get up and go out to do house calls during the night. She ought to try and sleep.

She went to bed with her book, and of course sleep deserted her so that she lay awake and read the same paragraph umpteen times while she listened to the water running and footsteps in Dan's room as he prepared for bed. Her visual imagination ran riot, which did nothing for her ability to sleep and even less for her blood pressure.

Finally all was quiet, and she put her book down and turned out her light. Sleep still eluded her, but she lay there in the dark and thought of Dan and wondered what it would take before he would let her get close to him.

Maybe he never would, she thought heavily. And maybe even though he was drawn to her physically he found her personality unattractive. There was nothing to say he had to like her. Why should he? OK, most people did, or seemed to, but Dan was under no obligation. Perhaps he was actually doing her a favour by pushing her away, if that was how he felt.

She punched her pillow, turned over to the other side and was just dozing off to sleep when she heard him groan. She sat bolt upright, listening carefully. A moment later it came again, a groan of pain, and her feet were on the floor and she was across the landing and in his room before she had time to reconsider.

He was lying on his back, sprawled diagonally across the big bed. His quilt had slipped half off, his pillow was sliding sideways the other way and his hands were buried in his hair. 'No-o,' he moaned, and Holly sat beside him on the edge of the bed and placed her hands gently over his.

'Dan?'

He went still, his body rigid for a second, then his hands fell to his sides and his eyes opened.

'What do you want?' he whispered hoarsely.

'You sounded as if you were in pain.'

He gave a tired grunt of laughter. 'Now there's a

thing,' he mumbled. 'I sound as if I'm in pain. What a surprise.'

'Is it your head?'

He nodded, his eyes glittering in the dim spill of yellow light that cut across from the open door. 'Yes,' he whispered. 'It's my head.'

'Migraine?'

He nodded. 'I've got some pills somewhere, but I couldn't focus. Don't want to take the wrong lot.' He gestured towards the bedside chest, and she opened a drawer and found migraine tablets in there—and half a packet of condoms. She shut the drawer quickly, popped a couple of the tablets out of the blister pack and handed them to him with the glass of water that was on the top.

He swallowed them, and fell back against the pillows with a groan. 'I'll be fine,' he whispered, but she could see the fine sheen of sweat on his skin.

She fetched a flannel from his bathroom and bathed his face with cool water, held a bowl as he retched helplessly and bathed his face again. It was a pattern she was to repeat a couple more times before he fell into a restless sleep.

She stayed with him until he was quiet and she was sure he was better, then she crept out and went back to her chilly bed. Her feet were like ice and if it hadn't been for the horrendous tongue-lashing she'd have got she'd have snuggled in beside him, but she didn't think getting that agitated would be good for him—and, besides, when she finally got into bed with Dan Elliott she wanted him sober, alert and very much aware of what was going on!

CHAPTER SEVEN

MONDAY morning started early, with a caller to the surgery at six o'clock. A middle-aged man, he looked at Holly as she opened the surgery door to him and he faltered.

'Oh. Um, is Dr Elliott about?'

'I'm afraid not. I'm doing the emergency surgery this morning. Come on in. What's the problem?'

He looked uncomfortable, and she wondered if it was a personal problem—something exclusively masculine that he wanted to see a male doctor about, for instance.

It wasn't. It was chest pain, similar to angina but not, Holly thought, anything to do with his heart. He had eaten heavily late last night, and she thought it was almost certain that he had simply given himself indigestion. However, with a man in his late forties she wasn't taking any chances, and while she took a history she had him sitting with an angina tablet under his tongue to see if it relieved the pain.

It didn't, as she had expected it wouldn't, and she gave him a thorough check over and then attached the electrodes to his wrists, ankles and chest for an ECG.

She'd go over it with Dan later, but at first glance it seemed quite normal, with all wavelengths as they should be and certainly no evidence of a recent heart attack.

She removed the electrodes, wiped up the contact jelly and smiled at him. 'Well, it looks OK, Mr Evans,' she told him cheerfully. 'Nothing drastic, certainly. I'll have a chat to Dr Elliott and go over the trace with him and then, if you come in and see him later for the result, you can talk it over with him, but I think you've got acid reflux—indigestion, simply.'

He looked even more worried. 'I don't need to take anything for that, do I?' he asked, almost comically concerned.

'No—not if you don't want to. I'd recommend a simple antacid preparation initially.'

Relief seemed to flood his face, and suddenly Holly realised the reason. Mrs Peake had come to her with a form of indigestion, and she'd ended up in hospital after an emergency tracheotomy on the kitchen table. No wonder the poor man was worried!

She sent him on his way and wondered how many other people were going to look at her like that today. Should she just hang out a sign that said, 'Dr Blake on duty. Don't bother to come'?

She made Dan a cup of tea and took it up to him. He was fast asleep, the strain of the night showing in the harsh lines etched on his face.

She opened the curtains a little and he stirred. She sat on the edge of the bed, her hip nudging his. 'Morning,' she said softly.

His eyes cracked open and he groaned. 'Already?'

'Mmm. I've brought you a cup of tea. How are you feeling?'

He struggled to a sitting position, dragging the quilt up his chest and collapsing against the headboard. 'Drained. At least it was at night this time.'

She passed him the tea. 'Do you get them often?'

'Since I had the accident, all the time. Not as bad

as that, though. It hasn't been that bad for weeks.'

She looked down at her hands. 'Want me to do your surgery?'

He started to shake his head, then thought better of it. 'No. No, I'll be fine. What's the time?'

'Seven-thirty.'

'No emergencies?'

'Just one so far. A Mr Evans—chest pain. I ran an ECG to be on the safe side, but I think it's just indigestion. Funnily enough that worried him even more. I think he's heard about Mrs Peake.'

Dan sighed and handed her the empty cup. 'Is that going to haunt us?' he mumbled. 'We ought to ring up about her.'

'I did—last night. Her tongue's down, they've removed the trachy tube and she's coming home in a day or two.'

'Full of vitriol. She's a difficult woman at the best of times. Damn. Why did it have to be her?'

Holly laughed softly. 'Why did it have to be me? Why did it have to be any of us? But I don't think you need to worry about lasting damage to the practice. Mr Evans asked for you and was most upset you weren't available.'

'Especially when he found out he'd got indigestion!'

Dan's smile reached his eyes, and Holly felt a tight contraction in her chest. Lord, how she loved him. Already, after so short a time, just a smile could turn her to mush. And those eyes. . .

Her mouth curved in response to his and, without thinking, she bent forward and dropped a light kiss on his lips.

'I'm glad you're feeling better. Get up when you're

ready. I've let the dogs out and I'll take them for a walk in a minute. Perhaps we can juggle your surgery so you only have a short list and then you could take a wander over to Becky, if you feel up to it, and see how her whooping cough is now.'

He was staring up at her, not taking in a word she was saying, and in the thin winter light filtering through the window she could see the naked longing in his eyes. Just for the hell of it she bent forward and kissed him again, and her breasts pressed softly against one of his arms.

A defeated groan erupted in his throat, and his arms slid round her, easing her closer as his lips welded to hers. One hand flattened and glided over her hip and up under her jumper, cupping the soft, aching fullness of her breast, and she turned slightly to give him better access. Her head dropped back against his shoulder, and he tipped her across his lap so that his lips could come down and fasten on the hard little peak that was so desperate for the feel of his mouth.

It was indescribable. Holly gave a little cry as she felt her nipple engulfed by the heat of his mouth and then, with the first deep suckle, a sharp stab of desire took her breath away.

'Dan,' she whispered soundlessly, arching in his arms to press herself even closer to that wonderful, wicked mouth. Her bra was pushed out of his way and she felt the hot, moist flick of his tongue across the turgid peak.

A sob was torn from her lips, and he stilled instantly, then slowly, reluctantly, he kissed the soft swell of her breast with infinite tenderness and covered her.

'Damn it, Holly,' he whispered raggedly, and his mouth brushed hers with just the faintest pressure. His eyes closed and he fell back against the pillows, his face taut with need.

Holly struggled to a sitting position and tugged her jumper straight, then ran her hands through her hair. Her ponytail had escaped, the band lost somewhere in the midst of his tangled bedding, and her breasts felt swollen and tender. She closed her eyes and counted to a hundred, then opened them.

He was watching her, the longing even more fierce now but accompanied by determination.

'Holly, this is going nowhere,' he told her, his voice gruff and husky with need.

'So you keep saying.'

'It isn't.'

'No.'

'Holly—'

'Dan, forget it. Now, why don't you have a lie-in and let me do your surgery?'

'You're just trying to keep me in bed.'

She laughed and stood up, her legs like rubber bands with knots in them. Somehow she made it to the door. 'Hardly,' she quipped. 'The way they all keep looking at me this morning it will be a miracle if I survive till lunchtime.'

'I thought you'd only had one patient so far?'

'I have. It just felt like ten.'

He gave a hollow little laugh. 'I have days like that.'

'Go back to sleep,' she ordered. 'I'll send Amy or Julia up with some breakfast for you at ten.'

He grunted, but whether with dissent or assent she wasn't sure. She didn't have time to worry any more because the surgery bell had rung, signalling the arrival of another patient. Just in time she remembered to straighten her jumper and drag her hair into another ponytail band, and when she opened the door the patient smiled at her.

Good, she thought, one person at least who doesn't think I'm going to kill them off. . .

In fact, her reception that morning was mixed, and it was the strangest thing that seemed to lay the ghost of Mrs Peake's disastrous reaction. She came out of her consulting room and was crossing the waiting room to speak to Dan in the kitchen when she saw a familiar face.

'Mr Jarvis?'

The man smiled broadly, stood up and pumped her hand. 'Is it young Holly? My, you've grown up! Are you this Dr Blake I've come to see?'

She smiled at the Yorkshireman. 'That's me. I'm doing locum here for a while to give Dr Elliott a hand.'

'And very welcome, I should say. I'd heard the new locum was a Dr Blake, but it never occurred to me it would be Phillip's daughter! Thought you'd be too good for the likes of us and go on to be a surgeon or some-such—gather you did rather well at your exams.'

Holly blushed. 'Well, I passed them, anyway.'

'Passed them?' He laughed heartily. 'I'll say you passed them. Should have heard your father when he came to see my bull that week. That proud of you, he was. Mind you, there's no way Phillip would have a daughter that wasn't as skilled as him in her field. A GP, eh? Well, there's a thing, young Holly!'

He patted her hand. 'Better not hold you up—expect you've got important things to do. I'll see you in a bit.'

She smiled and turned towards the door leading to the kitchen, and as she walked away she heard him turn to his neighbour in the waiting room. 'Our vet's daughter—bright as a button she was as a child, and no mistake. The apple of her father's eye. Could have gone on to do anything she wanted, but she's here with us and mighty lucky we are, too.

'Don't know what all this rubbish is about Gloria Peake, but I do know if she hadn't drunk so much over the years she wouldn't have had indigestion in the first place, most likely. I expect her tongue swelled up like Pinnochio's nose grew!'

Holly hurried into the kitchen, trying not to chuckle out loud, and bumped straight into Dan's chest. He reached up and steadied her, then drew her back into the kitchen. 'What was that about?' he murmured.

'Old Stan Jarvis—he recognised me, and now he knows who I am he's telling everyone Gloria Peake's tongue swelled up for the same reason Pinnochio's nose grew!'

Dan chuckled. 'Wicked man. That's not very kind.'

Holly sobered. 'No, it's not, and it won't help me if she gets to hear about it.'

'You have to admit it's funny, though,' Dan added, the smile still playing round his mouth.

'I just wish I could be accepted because they like and trust me, and not because I'm my father's daughter. That's one of the problems of taking a job round here— they all knew me when I was in nappies, and I was in Young Farmers with half of their sons, and it's difficult to be an independent professional.'

'You should try coming from London with a father with a Harley Street practice. They treated me like a leper till—well, for a long while.' He took a mug out

of the dishwasher and washed it up while she pondered
his words.

Till what? she wondered. Till his wife left? It was an
easy bet that none of them had liked her. If she was as
bad as she sounded he was better off without her, but
he shouldn't be alone. Nobody should be alone, not all
the time. Everyone needed a friend—a lover.

And she desperately wanted to be his. While she had
sat up with him in the night it had been so easy to
imagine she had the right to touch him, to sponge down
his face and shoulders and straighten his pillow and
watch him as he slept.

He had finished with the mug now, and turned round
so she could see his face. She studied it briefly, and
decided he looked better.

'You've got your colour back,' she told him softly.

'Yes. I feel human again, thank God. I took the dogs
for a walk and checked Becky.'

'Is she OK?'

'Fine. Did you want to see me, by the way?'

'Yes, about this.' She handed him the rolled-up ECG
trace from Mr Evans's early visit. 'Would you have a
look at it for me? I think it looks fine, but after our
friend with the tongue I'm not taking any chances.'

He took it from her, swapping it for a cup of coffee
freshly poured from the jug. 'Here, stay and drink this
for a moment while I look at it.'

'I ought to go and see the patients—I've got several
out there waiting.'

'I'll come in a minute. Just hang on and drink that
and let me have mine, and I'll take half the surgery.'

So she sat with him and studied him as he studied
the ECG, and because he had to take his dark glasses

off to see it clearly she was able to get a really close look at his eyes. It really was a crime to cover them, she decided. The lashes were positively sinful, and she wished he'd look up so she could stare into those gorgeous granite-blue depths and lose herself again.

Then she got her wish, and her legs turned back into the knotted rubber band variety as their gazes locked.

'What?' he said, cocking his head on one side.

She smiled. 'Just enjoying the view,' she told him.

His eyes heated again, and she knew it wouldn't be long before he gave in and surrendered to his feelings. She just hoped she could cope with the fall-out when he did.

She drained her coffee, slid the chair back and stood up. 'Coming?'

He grunted something unintelligible, and followed her through to the surgery. The waiting patients all smiled at her and nodded, and she wondered what Mr Jarvis had said to them after she was out of earshot.

Julia eyed her curiously, too. A farmer's daughter and fiancée of another farmer, Holly imagined that Julia knew Phillip Blake even if he wasn't their vet. Was her father's reputation in the area to be the only defence she needed? What about her own ability?

Damn. She'd avoided working in the area for just this reason, and now it seemed it was going to be the only thing to rescue her in the eyes of the patients.

She was right, they had had a change of attitude. Most of them knew her father, the others knew of him and she discovered he was universally liked and respected.

She also discovered that that was not enough. Fine, she belonged in their community. So far as that mattered, they were happy. As regards her professional ability and qualifications they were still wary, still hesitant after what had happened to Gloria Peake, and she would still have to prove herself as a doctor.

Fine. That suited her much better, and she perked up again and stopped worrying. She had no fears about her ability. Dan had checked the ECG and agreed with her that it was normal. He'd contacted Mr Evans, spoken to him and discovered that he had taken a simple antacid and was feeling much better, if a little flatulent.

He popped his head round the door between patients to tell her, and also told her that Mrs Peake was coming home the next day and had been assured by the hospital staff that her reaction was extremely rare, with under fifty cases reported nationally in the lifetime of the drug.

'They also told her,' he said with a grin, 'that if it hadn't been for the quick action of the primary medical team she would have died, and that she was very lucky to have had us there to act so promptly!'

Holly sat back in her chair and smiled wryly. 'Did they indeed? Well, bless their hearts.'

'It's true, you know. She would have died, and I wouldn't have got to her in time without you.'

'And would you have prescribed the same drug?'

'Inevitably. I've prescribed it this morning—it's a very useful drug. Come on, hurry up with your last patient and I'll take you over to the pub for lunch. I owe you after last night.'

'What about visits?'

'There aren't any. They've all been in bar a couple of local ones, and I've just done them on foot while you were doing the emergency surgery session. Now jump to it, I'm starving.'

She jumped. Within minutes they were tucked up by

the log fire in the pub on the other side of the village green, drinking freshly brewed coffee with thick swirls of cream on top while they browsed through the menu.

Dan was the first to decide. He slapped the menu shut, dropped it on the table and leant back, stretching out his long legs by the fire. 'Crispy mushrooms and bacon on toast, followed by raspberry pavlova, I think. What about you?'

She gave up wading through the range of goodies on offer, all of which sounded too good to pass up. 'Sounds good to me.'

It was. It was wonderful, and sitting by the fireside with Dan in this newly jovial mood was more intoxicating than any alcohol would have been. The mobile phone didn't ring, either, and they wrapped up and strolled back across the green with an almost leisurely air.

It couldn't last, Holly thought, and as her foot touched the doorstep of the cottage she heard the phone ring inside. Julia was taking the call as they went in, and she looked at Dan strangely—almost pityingly.

What is it? Holly wondered. Something had happened. She had the most awful sinking feeling as they went into the office and Julia handed Dan a slip of paper.

'Somebody called Jocelyn rang. Could you call her back urgently, please, on that number?'

His face was like a mask, the colour drained from it in an instant. 'Did she say what it was about?'

Julia bit her lip. 'I didn't ask, but she sounded—well, a bit upset about something. She said something about Randolph?'

'My father. Damn. OK, thank you, Julia. Any other calls?'

She shook her head, and Dan disappeared into his

room, shutting the door behind him with a definite click. Holly, watching him go, felt her heart sink into her boots. Was his father dead? Dying? And how would he feel? She thought how she would feel if it was her father, and wanted to go to him.

This was Dan, though, and he did things his way. He wouldn't want her in there, and it was quite possible it was nothing important at all. Whatever, he would tell her in his own good time.

She went into the kitchen, determined not to allow her imagination to run away with her, and bumped into Mrs Hodges.

'Hello, dear,' the cheerful woman said. 'How's it going? I've changed your bed and put fresh towels out for you, and I've done Dr Elliott's bed—it was in a dreadful tangle. Was he ill again?'

She nodded. 'Yes—a migraine. He's all right now.'

Mrs Hodges tutted. 'Poor man, ever since he had that accident he's been such a restless sleeper. Still, can't be helped. Now, I've done you a nice chicken hotpot for tonight, and— Oh, Dr Elliott, whatever's the matter? You look terrible!'

He did. Holly crossed over to him and took his arm. 'Dan? What is it? What's happened?'

He looked down at her blankly for a moment, then pulled off the glasses and rubbed his eyes. He seemed shocked, she thought. 'Dan?' she prompted gently.

He looked at her, his eyes locking with hers as if he were hanging onto reality by a thread. 'My father's in hospital. He's had a heart attack. He wants to see me.'

'Then you must go,' she told him.

'Come with me. We'll get locum cover—Julia can arrange it.'

She stared at him in astonishment. Why would he want her? He hardly knew her. Surely there must be someone he knew better who could take him?

'Please,' he said simply, and she couldn't refuse him. 'Now?'

'We don't need to take anything. We'll be back by tonight.'

'But what if he's—'

'Dying? There won't be any painful deathbed scenes, Holly. My father and I are hardly the best of friends. He wants to see me. He'll see me, but not for long. Don't worry, there isn't going to be any harrowing breast-beating.'

'Don't be ridiculous,' she scolded gently. 'You don't know how you'll feel.'

He met her eyes again, and now his were composed and remote. 'Oh, yes, I do.' He put the glasses on again almost defiantly, and turned to Mrs Hodges. 'If you could leave whatever you've cooked in the fridge we can heat it up when we get home. Thanks, Mrs Hodges. Right, are you ready?'

Holly blinked. 'Yes, sure. I could do with a quick freshen up—'

'Come on, then. Ten minutes. I'll talk to Julia and get this cover arranged.'

And that was it. Holly visited the bathroom, freshened her make-up and met him downstairs in the office in eight minutes. They left almost immediately, driving down the M11 into London and then with Dan's directions cutting through the traffic and ending up outside a very smart looking Harley Street clinic just as the light was fading. 'Park round the back,' he instructed, and she turned down a narrow mews and into the space he indicated.

'Is he here?'

Dan shook his head. 'No. It's his clinic. He's a few doors up in another one. We'll walk.'

It was hardly any distance, but with every step Holly could sense Dan's reluctance growing. How much could he hate this man? It seemed impossible to do anything but love one's father, but then they weren't all like hers. She looked up at him, but in the shadowy yellow light of the streetlamps his face looked totally impassive.

They stopped outside the entrance to a clinic, and Holly looked up at the impressive building and her heart sank. How rich was Dan—or was it all his father's money? She felt totally out of her depth, her clothes shabby and ordinary—her coat definitely not this year's fashion. Still, that wasn't why she was here. She was here to give Dan moral support—she thought. She wasn't even sure of that any more.

He straightened his shoulders, reached for her hand and squeezed it, and then ushered her up the steps to the entrance.

A receptionist, cool, elegant and composed, looked up from her station behind a desk and smiled a welcome. 'Can I help you?' she murmured in a beautifully modulated voice.

'I'm here to see Dr Elliott.'

'Ah, yes. You must be his son—we were told to expect you. If you could take a seat for a moment I'll get someone to show you to his room.'

Holly perched on the edge of a pale gold buttoned chair. Dan prowled, poking the plants and generally betraying his restlessness. He was nervous, she realised suddenly, and wondered why. What sort of man was his father?

A pretty girl in nurse's uniform appeared and greeted them, then led them along a corridor and up a flight of stairs to the floor above. At the end of another corridor she ushered them into a room, smiled sweetly and left them.

For what seemed like an age Dan stood motionless, then there was a little cry of anguish and a flurry of arms and legs and a slender cobweb of a woman threw herself into Dan's arms.

At least she tried to, but he caught her by the shoulders and moved her back, his face a mask of disapproval.

'Hello, Jocelyn,' he said, and his voice was dead and cold. His eyes were concealed by the glasses, but the room was dimly lit anyway. Holly looked around at the expensive decor, the lush pile carpet, the designer curtains, and then at the bed set in the centre of the far wall like a jewel in a crown.

Huge floral arrangements swamped the bedside table and stood on the floor, artfully disguising the trailing tubes and wires connected to the built-in monitor and oxygen supply set in the wall behind the bedhead.

The other end of the tubes and wires led to the man who lay sleeping on the bed, his dark hair silvered at the temples but otherwise very like his son. He looked frail and tired with purple shadows under his eyes, and Holly was busy feeling sorry for him when his eyes flickered open and latched onto Dan like twin lasers.

'Took your time, didn't you, son?' he said, and his voice was like ice. Holly felt chilled by it, horrified by the lack of warmth and feeling.

'We came as soon as Jocelyn called,' Dan said stiffly. 'I gather you wanted to see me.'

'Yes. I wanted to see you to talk some sense into you. You'll have to come home. I can't run the practice any more. I need you here, where you belong.'

'No.'

'Daniel, you owe me—'

'I owe you nothing. I told you years ago I didn't want your money or any part of your life. I don't want your clinic, and I certainly am not about to abandon my patients to come back here and pander to the rich and spoiled plutocrats you indulge with your bogus nonsense.'

Mottled colour darkened the older man's cheeks. Holly, too, felt colour run over her skin but it was from shame—shame that Dan could speak like that to his father when the man was clearly so ill.

Then Jocelyn took Dan's arm and stroked it, all but rubbing herself against him. 'Please, Dan—he needs you. I need you—I miss you. He can't manage any more—'

'Can't manage what?'

The implication was so unsubtle that Holly's breath caught. Was she flirting with him—and who was she, anyway? Dan's father's mistress? His wife? Whatever, that was no way to speak to her, surely?

Jocelyn seemed to look at him and for the first time she stared at the scar that slashed across his cheek.

She reached out a trembling hand as if to touch him, but withdrew it just at the last minute. 'What—what happened?' she whispered.

'I had an accident.'

'You're disfigured!'

'Yes. My ribs are good, too—want to see them?'

'No!' She turned away, her hand pressed to her mouth, and crossed to Randolph's side. 'Darling, tell him not to tease me.'

Dan's face hardened again. 'Don't worry, we're going before I choke on the carpet pile. Do take care of yourself, won't you, Father—and Jocelyn, of course? She enjoys spending your money.'

'I'll cut you out of my will!' his father bellowed.

'Feel free. I told you to do that years ago,' Dan retorted and, turning on his heel, he took Holly's arm and steered her out of the room.

She went automatically, shocked by the lack of warmth and caring she had witnessed in that room. She was silent all the way back to the car, then she sat in the driver's seat and stared out of the windscreen.

'Why do you hate him so much?' she said finally.

'Because he's a faithless bastard, a womanising snake, a liar and a cheat.'

'And Jocelyn? What's she done to you that you're so unpleasant to her? Can't you even be civil to his wife?'

Dan turned towards her, and she could see his features clearly in the harsh glare of the security lights.

'His wife? Oh, no, Holly, that's not his wife. Furthermore she can't be as long as I or my mother are alive. It's against the law.'

'Against the law?' she repeated, utterly lost. 'How can it be against the law?'

'Because she's *my* wife—or was. That, Holly dear, is the ex Mrs Daniel Elliott.'

CHAPTER EIGHT

'YOUR wife?' Holly whispered incredulously. 'Jocelyn was your wife?'

Dan sighed. 'Yes. Now can you see why I don't like to talk about her?'

Only too clearly, Holly thought, stunned by his revelation. She tried to imagine how she would feel if Dan started to have an affair with her mother, and found the whole train of thought too painful and distasteful to consider—and they weren't even involved in an intimate relationship yet. No wonder Dan had no time for the woman!

'How—? When—? Oh, Dan, I'm so sorry,' she finally managed.

He gave a hollow laugh. 'You and me both. I have to admit it was a bit of a shock when I found out. Not that it exactly surprised me that either of them would sink so low, but one always hopes. Still. It's over now, I don't have to see them and, frankly, life's easier that way. Shall we get back?'

Holly couldn't wait. She couldn't shrug off London and its money and artifice and scheming lies quickly enough.

It was nearly midnight by the time they drew up outside the practice in Wiventhorpe, and Holly had never been so pleased to be anywhere in her life. The sitting-room lights were on, and when they went in they found Julia and her fiancé watching television, the dogs and the cat sprawled happily by the fire.

'How is he?' Julia asked, getting to her feet.

'He'll live. Thanks for dog-sitting. How's the evening been?'

'Fine. I cancelled everything that wasn't important, scaled down the surgery and Dr Roberts came over for an hour to cover the emergencies. I'm glad you're back, though, because tomorrow looks horrendous.'

Dan smiled tiredly. 'Yes, we're back. Thanks, Julia. Thanks, Peter.'

He showed them out, then went into the kitchen and poured himself a slosh of malt whisky in the bottom of a glass. 'Join me?' he offered.

'I'm on call.'

'No, you're not. I've got the on-call co-op covering tonight, to be on the safe side. We take over again at eight tomorrow morning—so do you want a whisky?'

She smiled. 'Go on, then, just a small one.'

He sloshed a similar amount into another glass, and handed it to her. 'Here—and thank you, Holly.'

'My pleasure. I'm just sorry it was such an awful day for you.'

He gave a mirthless grunt of laughter. 'Seeing my father is enough to ruin any day. I've tried hard to forgive him for what he did to my mother but, frankly, I don't think the man deserves or wants forgiveness. He's a manipulator, but I think he's finally getting his comeuppance.

'He only stole Jocelyn from me out of spite because I refused to work in his damn clinic, but I don't think he'll keep her for long now. She's getting bored and restless, and obviously he's not able to deliver the goods any longer as far as their sex life is concerned. That's why she wants me back—or did until she saw the scars.'

'Oh, Dan.' Holly set her glass down untouched, and without hesitation she went over to him, took off his glasses and put them down, then pulled his face down to hers. She laid her lips along the line of the scar and a shudder went through him.

It was much more than her touch, she knew that. It was the culmination of a long and difficult day, and she lifted his head a fraction and turned her face so that her lips brushed his. 'Forget her, Dan. She's not worth worrying about.'

His mouth twisted in a lopsided smile. 'That's what my mother says—she describes her as a waste of a good skin.' His arms tightened round her, and his eyes looked down into hers and she was lost.

His lips were gentle, his kiss a tender caress that spoke volumes. After a moment he lifted his head and stared down at her.

'I want you, Holly,' he murmured.

'I know.'

'Now. Tonight.'

She stared into those gorgeous grey eyes shot through with sapphire, and she couldn't have refused him anything.

'Yes,' she said simply.

The breath left his lungs with a rush, and he took her by the hand and led her silently up the stairs. Her heart was pounding, her lungs felt as if they would burst and yet she couldn't have turned back to save her life.

He left her at the bathroom door with a gentle kiss. 'I just have to go and sort the dogs out, make a couple of phone calls and then I'll be up, but I could do with a shower. Why don't you go first?'

She did, washing away the smell and taste and feel of London, and after she had scrubbed every inch of her skin until it glowed she towelled herself dry, dabbed a little scent discreetly on her pulse points and wondered what the form was now. Did she go and wait in his bed? Or hers? Or neither? Was she supposed to hover enticingly in a negligee? If so, he was doomed to disappointment because she didn't own one and there was no way she was fairying about dressed like that in January for anyone!

The water was running in Dan's bathroom so he was obviously only a few minutes behind her. She went into her bedroom, put on a clean cotton nightshirt and her towelling dressing gown, and sat down to brush the tangles out of her hair.

Her heart racing with anticipation, she heard the water stop, the click of his bathroom door and then she watched in the mirror as he appeared in the doorway behind her dressed in his towelling robe. His hair was still damp, his legs hastily dried and still beaded with water, and she had a sneaking suspicion that the bits in between had been swiped with a towel at the same speed. She wondered if he would make a grab for her, if this first time would be ruined by his impatience, but it seemed he was only impatient to be with her.

He came up behind her, his eyes locking with hers in the mirror. He took the brush from her hand and started to brush out her hair, the strokes long and lazy as if they had all the time in the world.

'So beautiful,' he murmured. His hands sifted the heavy strands, and her eyes half closed, almost hypnotised by the rhythmic movement.

Then he let her hair fall and, taking her hand, he lifted her hand to his lips.

'Come to bed,' he said softly.

She stood up, her knees almost useless, and if he hadn't put his arm round her and drawn her to his side she would have fallen over. She slid an arm round his waist for support and as they walked into his room she was conscious of an overwhelming feeling of rightness that drove out any lingering doubts she might have had.

Pausing by the bed in the shadowed room, he turned her in his arms and looked down at her, his eyes hidden from her by the darkness. She wanted the lights on, wanted to see him as he loved her, but she didn't like to ask and, anyway, she might feel different later on. Perhaps she would feel shy with him when it came to the crunch.

She said nothing, and seconds later she was glad she had because he tugged the belt of her dressing-gown loose, tucked his hands into the open edges at the neck and slid it back over her shoulders so that it puddled at her feet.

He smiled then. 'Rabbits?' he said laughingly, his fingers tracing the gambolling bunnies on the front of her nightshirt. 'How appropriate.'

Taking the hem in his hands, he peeled it over her head and left her standing naked in front of him. Dropping the nightshirt, he let his eyes roam over her— feasting on her. At least that was what it felt like to Holly, stark naked and achingly vulnerable as he studied every inch of her body in silence.

Then he lifted his hands and took her hair, arranging it so that it fell like a curtain over her breasts, his hands trembling as he did so. Could he really want her so badly he was shaking? Apparently. Unsure what to do, she stood there motionless until finally he lifted his head and met her eyes, and even in the dark she could see the glitter of desire in their depths.

'Dear God, Holly,' he whispered. She could see his chest rising and falling rapidly, and hear the soft rush of his breath as he gazed longingly at her.

What was she supposed to do? How long could she stand there?

She couldn't. She wanted to see him, touch him, hold him. Her hands reached out, trembling, and undid the belt of his towelling robe and then, as he had done to her, she slid it off his shoulders and let it fall.

She nearly went with it, the tension was so great. Her hands lingered on his shoulders, feeling the heat of the powerful flesh beneath her palms, the firm tone of the muscles, the satin smoothness of the skin.

She slid her hands down over his chest and felt the rough, uneven lines of scar tissue over his ribcage. His breath caught, locking in his throat as she stroked and searched out the scars. 'Oh, Dan,' she whispered. 'You must have been so hurt.'

She didn't know if she was talking about his accident or his wife, but it didn't matter. Her words broke the tension, and with a gruff cry he wrapped her in his arms and drew her hard up against his body. His mouth found hers, locking on it as one hand cradled her breast and the other slid down and cupped her bottom, lifting her hard against him.

She felt the solid thrust of his erection, hard and hot against her softness, and with a whimper she rocked against him, desperate to close the gap and be a part of him.

He groaned her name, lifted her, laid her on the bed and came down beside her, one hard thigh thrust between hers, his lips laying a trail of hot, open-mouthed kisses over her neck and shoulders.

He found her breasts, soothing the ache with his hands and tongue, then building it still higher as she squirmed helplessly against him. His hands moved lower, seeking out the focus of the ache, tormenting her with slow, gliding strokes that made her cry out with need.

There was a moment's fumbled pause as he remembered to protect her, then he moved over her, trapped her head between his hands and stared deep into her eyes. Then he shifted his hips and there was an almost unbearable fullness as their bodies locked together, and Holly cried out his name on a sobbing breath and buried her head in his shoulder.

It was too much—too powerful, too wonderful, too intense to bear. He held her for a moment as if he understood, then slowly, gently, he started to move. The tension eased a little, then wound tighter again and tighter, until with a gasp of surprise Holly felt the world splinter all around her and vanish in an eddy of white heat.

Dan cried out, a harsh guttural cry of release, and then his body slumped against her, his passion spent, his strength totally drained. Her arms were weak still, but they crept round him and held him against her heart and her eyes filled with tears.

So that was what it was like. She had expected pain, perhaps, although probably not much. She had hoped for pleasure but, again, probably not much, at least not the first time.

Never in her wildest dreams had she dreamt of anything so beautiful, so consuming, so powerful.

Dan lifted his head and stared down at her, then his fingertips stroked the tears from her cheeks. 'Did I hurt you?' he murmured, his brow gathering in a little frown of concern.

'No. I thought you might, but, no, it was wonderful. Thank you, Dan.'

He laughed self-consciously. 'Don't thank me, Holly. The pleasure was all mine.'

'I don't think so.' She touched his face, her fingertips light over the fine lines and shattered bone. 'I love you, Dan.'

He froze for a second, then his eyes slid shut and he dropped his head against her shoulder. 'No, Holly.'

'Yes, Dan. Why not?'

'Because I can't love you back.'

'No, you won't.'

'Holly, I can't—and, you're right, I won't. You just think you love me. It's because it was great sex. It's always the same. You know that.'

She turned her head so she could see him in the dim light. 'How should I know that? I've never done it before.'

If she thought he was still before he was utterly transfixed now. 'Never?' he finally managed in a strangled voice. 'You've never made love before?'

She shook her head.

'With anyone?'

'No.'

'But—why not?'

She shrugged. 'Never seemed worth it before. I've had boyfriends, of course, but it's never seemed right.

They were nice guys, but there didn't seem to be any point, really. Not till you.'

His eyes searched hers, his expression wary. 'So, why me? What makes me different, Holly?'

'You just are.' Her fingers cupped his cheek lovingly. 'Nobody else has ever given me that forever feeling before.'

'Forever feeling?' he whispered. 'What forever feeling? Holly, there is no forever.' He levered himself up and away from her, swinging his legs over the side of the bed and leaving her bereft. 'Damn it, Holly, you should have told me it was your first time.'

'So you could have done the decent thing and refused to make love to me? Not a chance, Dan. That was the most wonderful experience in my life, and if you imagine I would have given it up to protect your finer feelings you can forget it.'

She knelt up in the middle of the bed, her hands on his shoulders, and squeezed the taut muscles gently. 'Lie down, Dan. It's too late to worry about my virginity and, anyway, it's high time I lost it. The damn thing was becoming a nuisance.'

He half turned his head. 'How can something so closely guarded become a nuisance?'

He was right, of course. Her virginity had never been a nuisance. It was her reluctance to involve herself with anyone she didn't truly love that had been the nuisance, if you could call it that.

She clucked at him. 'Don't fuss. It's over now. Lie down on your front, let me give you a massage. You're all tense.'

For a moment he sat there, rigid with tension, then with a tattered sigh he lay down and she sat astride his thighs and smoothed her hands up his back. The skin was too dry so she hopped off the bed and went to her room, then came back with a bottle of baby lotion. Arranging herself over his thighs again, she warmed a dollop of the lotion in her hands, smeared it over his skin and began the long, slow strokes up the length of his back.

He groaned softly and settled himself more comfortably, and under her hands she felt the tension go out of him. Good. He'd had a horrendous day, and he'd given her more pleasure than she could ever have expected. It was no hardship to return the favour.

She moved down, kneeling beside his legs as she worked the lotion down over the hair-strewn skin. His right thigh was a little thinner, and up the outside of it was a fine scar. There was another on his hip, a legacy of the pin that held his leg together—more evidence of his damaged body. She worked the tight, knotted muscles of his right thigh gently, feeling the tension return to him as she touched the tender areas.

'Does that hurt?'

'No. I'm just erring on the safe side,' he said drily, and she laughed and moved to the other leg.

'Better?' she asked, and he mumbled his agreement.

She reached his feet, massaging the soles with her thumbs, and then she sat back and patted him on his firm, taut bottom.

'All done.'

He rolled over onto his side and lay there looking up at her, his face in shadow. 'Come here,' he said gruffly, and she lay down facing him, just inches away. His hands came up and cupped her cheeks, and he kissed her gently on the mouth. 'Holly, I'm going to hurt you,' he said softly.

Her eyes filled with tears. 'Probably—but not before you've made me happier and more fulfilled than I've ever been in my life.'

His face creased with anguish. 'Holly, why me? Of all the men in the world, why pick on such a loser?'

'You're not a loser, Dan.'

He gave a dismissive grunt of laughter. 'Of course I am. I'm an emotional cripple, Holly, not to mention the mess my body's in.'

'It looks pretty good to me.'

'In the dark.'

'So turn the lights on.'

'No. Leave me my dignity, Holly, for God's sake.'

Sorrow welled inside her at his words. 'Oh, Dan.' She closed the gap between them, burying her face in his shoulder so he wouldn't see her tears, and pressed her lips to his throat. 'I don't care about your scars,' she whispered sadly. 'I just need to hold you.'

His chest heaved, as if he was struggling with a wave of emotion, and his fingers caught her chin and tipped her mouth up to meet his, and there was nothing else to say.

His loving was so gentle this time, so tender and careful that she thought she'd die of frustration. He built her to fever pitch before he moved across her and took her desperate, frenzied body with his own, and as the endless waves of her climax slowly died away the tears welled helplessly from her eyes and she bit her lip to trap the sobs.

Then Dan lifted his head and kissed her tears away,

and she hugged him close and didn't care if he knew what he did to her.

She belonged here with him, with this proud, wounded man who was too afraid to love. However much he might fight it, they were meant to be together and she would die before she gave up on him.

She knew what tonight was all about. That was fine. She understood his pain and frustration and anguish over his father and Jocelyn, and if he was only turning to her for comfort, so what? It was a start. They had to begin somewhere. At least, for now, he was letting her close to him. She'd just have to make sure he didn't shut her out again once the first heat of passion cooled.

If it hadn't been for the dogs they would have overslept, but they whined and scratched at the kitchen door and the sound gradually penetrated the sensuous haze that surrounded Dan and Holly.

Dan threw back the covers and sat up, stretching gloriously and wondering when he had last felt so human. Humming, he picked up his robe off the floor, shoved his arms into the sleeves, belted it hastily and ran downstairs to let the dogs out and put the kettle on. It was ten to eight and, with a full surgery starting at eight-thirty and Julia and Amy due in at a quarter past, they didn't have long to get ready for the fray.

Leaving the dogs outside to romp in the remains of the snow, he ran upstairs and woke Holly with a quick shake and a peck on the cheek. 'Come on, lazybones, time to get up.'

She rolled onto her back and stretched, and the quilt pulled down to reveal her soft, ripe breasts flushed pink with the warmth of the bed. He groaned inwardly, want-

ing nothing more than to climb back under the covers
with her and lose himself in that glorious body all
over again.

Instead he buried his fist in the quilt, whisked it off
her and treated himself to two seconds of whirling limbs
and flying hair before he ran into the bathroom and
slammed the door just as she hurled herself against it,
fists flailing.

'That is the pits, Dan Elliott!' she yelled, and he
chuckled and turned the shower on flat out and stepped
under the glorious hot blast. Lord, she was beautiful,
slim and yet full, her body curving generously in all the
right places. And those legs! His body clenched with
the memory of them locked tightly round him, and he
dropped his head against the tiled wall and swore softly.

He couldn't wait to make love to her again. He wondered despairingly if he would ever grow tired of it and,
if not, how he would learn to live without it—and her—
when she woke up to the reality of a GP's life in the
depths of rural Norfolk, miles from the shops and anything smacking of culture.

Holly, though, was used to it, he thought, and then
chastised himself for tormenting his hopelessly optimistic heart with such fruitless encouragement.

She'd go. Even if the place was all right, being trapped
with a morose cripple with a body like a road map was
enough to put any self-respecting woman off.

And she had yet to see him in daylight, of course. . .

Holly opened the door to the waiting room just seconds
before Julia and Amy arrived. She was in the kitchen,
feeding the dogs and making toast, when they came
in and they looked around to check that Dan wasn't

there before they asked Holly how he was.

'Have you seen each other this morning?' Julia asked her.

Well, Dan had certainly seen her. Holly fought down the wave of colour. 'Yes—um, I think he's all right. We haven't really talked. I don't think his father's condition was that serious after all so I don't imagine he'll be that worried.' She didn't know how much they knew about Jocelyn or his father, and it was hardly her place to tell them, so she busied herself with a piece of toast and they made some tea and left the room, to her great relief.

When Dan came in moments later she told him Julia had been asking how he was.

He frowned. 'And?'

'I told her you were magnificent.'

He blushed. To her absolute astonishment, his neck turned brick red and he all but growled. 'Damn it, Holly, be serious.'

'I am,' she said softly, and his breath jerked out of his body and he screwed up his hand into a fist and looked around for somewhere to plant it. 'Don't hit me,' she said with a laugh, and his mouth softened into a slight curve.

'So, what did you say to Julia?'

'I told her you were all right as far as I knew. I said your father didn't seem to be that seriously ill.'

'Well, he's not critical, and he'd be a damn sight better if he'd stop drinking and if he had a clean conscience.' He gave a hollow laugh. 'On second thoughts, I don't think his conscience probably troubles him at all.'

He helped himself to the other half of her toast and bit into it, then swallowed half her tea.

'I don't suppose you want my patients as well, do you?' she offered.

His chuckle followed him out of the room and down the hall towards the waiting room, which was already filling up. With a smile Holly followed him, went into her room and called the first patient.

It was a busy day, not surprisingly, as so many of the appointments had been reshuffled from the day before. She finished her routine surgery and then went out on calls, leaving Dan to pick up the emergency surgery cases and the walking wounded. Typically, there were several calls from people who had chosen not to be seen by the strange practice who had been on call for them overnight, and so Holly found herself straggling about all over the county, or so it seemed.

It was three before she got back to the practice, and Dan was halfway through his routine antenatal clinic with Amy. Julia collared Holly and waved a note at her. 'Mrs Peake—she's back home and needs a visit. Dan asked if you wanted to go now, or on the other hand you could wait for him to finish and go together.'

Holly rolled her eyes and took the note, scanning it. 'Does she have a problem or is it a routine discharge visit?'

Julia shrugged. 'She didn't say. I expect it's just routine—a woman like that expects to be waited on.'

'Did she ask for Dan?'

'No, actually.' Julia smiled. 'She asked for you.'

'Me? Oh, Lord, she probably wants to tell me personally that she's going to sue me.'

Julia shook her head. 'Oh, no. When she sued the butcher for a piece of gristle in her sausage-meat which broke her dentures she had the solicitor write to him. I don't think she's going to sue you. Actually, she sounded quite perky.'

Holly took a deep breath and shrugged. 'I'll go now. If I wait for Dan the suspense will kill me.'

She got back in the car and drove the short distance to the Peakes' house, and was greeted at the door by a smiling Mr Peake. 'Dr Blake—come on in,' he said, and ushered her into the drawing room.

Mrs Peake was reclining on the sofa with a scarf draped round her throat, no doubt to disguise the tracheotomy incision, and she reached out a hand to Holly and beckoned her over. Holly perched on the sofa at her feet.

'Hello, Mrs Peake. You're looking a bit better than when I last saw you,' she said, and waited for the bomb to drop.

The woman rolled her eyes. 'Oh, yes, thank God,' she said fervently. Her voice was a little raspy and her tongue seemed thickened still, but she was very much alive and well—and apparently grateful. 'I owe you my life, it seems,' she told her. 'Now, I know I can't give you any money because it's against the laws of ethics or somesuch, but I wanted you to know I don't hold any grudge because of my drug reaction and I'm just so grateful to you and Dr Elliott for saving my life that I want you to have this.'

She handed her an envelope, and Holly put it down on her lap and stared at it. 'Look, Mrs Peake, I don't know what this is but I really don't feel we deserve anything,' she said quietly. 'If I hadn't prescribed that drug you would have been fine.'

'Oh, tosh. I'd overeaten, anyway. It was my own fault. Please, Dr Blake, do accept it.'

'Only if you accept my apology for what happened.'

Their eyes met, and after a moment Mrs Peake patted her hand. 'There's no need to apologise but, if it makes you feel happier, I accept.'

'Thank you,' Holly opened the envelope and drew out a thank-you card. Folded inside it was a restaurant menu with a note attached, saying that a meal for two had been paid for and could be taken at any time in the next month.

'You'll have to take a night off together and go and indulge yourselves,' she said imperiously, and ruined it by smiling a little tearfully and patting Holly's hand. 'I'm so grateful to you both—please don't go and spoil my treat by arguing and shoving ethics down my throat. I've had enough down there in the last couple of days to last me a lifetime!'

Holly put the card down and took Mrs Peake's hand, squeezing it gently. 'Thank you. You're very kind, and it's most appreciated. Neither of us can cook for nuts, and if it wasn't for Mrs Hodges we'd probably starve, so you really have chosen a wonderful treat. It really wasn't necessary, but I'm not going to turn it down because it looks so delicious and I know it's a fabulous place.'

'Just mind you don't overdo it and end up with indigestion!'

Holly laughed with her, and then asked how her original problem was.

'Oh, a little better, I think. They gave me something else in hospital to clear it up, and it seems to have done the trick for now—but they also gave me a stiff lecture on smoking, drinking, eating too much and being overweight. I asked if I would live for ever if I did as they said and they said, no, it would just feel like it.'

Holly chuckled and patted Mrs Peake's hand. 'I'm sure it won't be that bad, and you know it's sound advice. Oesophagitis is usually easy to cure if you don't persistently aggravate it by overdoing things.'

'So I've been told,' the woman said drily. 'Well, I won't hold you up any longer, dear, but I just wanted you to know I don't hold it against you and I'm very glad I'm alive to say so.'

'And so am I.'

Holly left her, the card and menu clutched in her hand, and drove back to the surgery. It was almost four and Dan was just making a cup of tea when she arrived back.

'Perfect timing,' he said over his shoulder. 'What did she want?'

Holly handed him the card and took the tea he pushed towards her.

He gave a low whistle. 'Dinner at the Badger's Rest? She must be nuts—or even more grateful than I'd imagined.'

'That's what I thought. My parents went there once a couple of years ago for their thirtieth wedding anniversary. They said it was wonderful.'

'It is. We'll go on Saturday—it's the anniversary of my crash. We can celebrate my survival.'

She decided to ignore the rather bitter tone to his voice and take the statement at face value. She smiled. 'Sounds good. Can you get the practice covered?'

'Yes—and we'll have a taxi. That way you can drink.' He looked down at the card and smiled wryly. 'Good old Mrs Peake. Who would have thought she had it in her? Just goes to show how coming face to face with your own mortality makes you reassess your priorities.'

As he had?

He'd certainly come face to face with his mortality a year ago. Holly wondered what difference it had made to his life—and whether it had made him even harder to reach. . .

CHAPTER NINE

HOLLY thought Saturday would never come. They were incredibly busy for the rest of that week, as if fate wanted to make sure that they had no time to be alone together.

For Holly, who wanted nothing more than to be with Dan, it was unbearable. She also felt that it didn't serve her purpose as she'd intended to get in there so close to him and so consistently that he became used to her presence in his life and found it indispensable to his happiness.

Fate wasn't playing ball. Two more children from Becky's class in the local primary school went down with whooping cough, and although they were not as bad as she had been they were still whooping well and Dan and Holly kept a close eye on them. Flu was doing its usual winter rounds, and although they both remained free of it for the time being the number of patients struck down with it and its follow-on infections meant Holly was kept constantly on the run with her outside calls.

'How on earth did you ever cope alone?' she asked him on Wednesday night as she got back in from a call at eleven-thirty, just as he was shutting the door on another emergency patient.

He laughed wryly. 'Did I ever say I coped?'

'Now you come to mention it, no. I'm shattered and I've only been here for a week. You must have the constitution of an ox.'

'Sheer bloodymindedness, more like.' He drew her

149

into his arms in the kitchen and was just lowering his head to kiss her when the phone rang again.

He sighed, released her and picked up the receiver. 'Dr Elliott.'

Holly waited. There was no point in taking off her coat and scarf and gloves and boots just to have to put the whole lot back on again seconds later.

Dan was jotting something down. 'By all means come on in and I'll have a look at you,' he said. 'No, I don't mind at all. How soon can you get here? Ten minutes? Fine. I'll see you then.'

Holly took off her clobber, dropped into a chair and propped her chin in her hands. 'One for you?'

'Yes. Mr Evans. His chest pain's bad again.'

Holly chewed her lip. 'Perhaps we should admit him for tests. Maybe it's not indigestion after all.'

'Maybe it's not. He might have a stomach ulcer or oesophagitis, or perhaps he really does have a heart condition and it's just not showing up on the ECG. I'll see what he comes up with tonight.'

Holly, too, was very interested as she had seen him first on Monday and had performed the initial ECG. However, shortly after Mr Evans arrived, Holly had to go out on another call, and by the time she came back it was well after midnight and Dan had gone to bed.

It seemed like a fine idea so, after letting the dogs out for a last run, she went upstairs to find Dan's door open.

'Holly?' he called softly.

She went in and sat on the edge of the bed. 'Hi. How was Mr Evans?'

Dan shrugged. 'Seemed fine. I couldn't find anything wrong with him, but he says the pain's severe and the way he describes it I'm not prepared to take the risk.

He's not especially fit, his lifestyle isn't overwhelmingly healthy and what with one thing and another I just don't want to gamble on it.'

'Good.' Holly grinned. 'We don't need another Mrs Peake. Let someone else make the difficult decisions. What do you think's wrong, by the way?'

'Pass. I'll refer him with central chest pain and let them decide. I've told him to come in tomorrow morning and I'll send him in with a letter. It could be cardiac neurosis.'

'That's unlikely, isn't it?'

'But possible. Anyway, after tomorrow morning it'll be someone else's worry. They've got the equipment and facilities to investigate. We can really only guess and I don't want to do that, not with a potentially fatal condition.'

'I wonder why not?' she said with a grin. 'Right, I'm going to bed. With any luck I might get some sleep before the next call.'

Dan's laugh followed her down the landing and into her bedroom. She would rather have been with him but he hadn't invited her, and as the chances were she'd be up half the night it wasn't really fair. Instead, she lay in bed and thought about him, and how it would be if she was in his arms instead of between her own not nearly so welcoming sheets, and it was almost a relief when the phone rang again.

It was Mrs Evans, to say that her husband was pacing round in pain again, couldn't lie down and she wanted something done now.

Holly promised to be there as soon as possible, slid her legs out of bed and stood up nose to nose with Dan. 'Who is it?' he asked.

'Mr Evans. Want to come?'

'There's no point. You're just as qualified as I am—unless you'd rather I came?'

'Are you going to lie awake until I get back?'

'Probably.'

'Then come. I'll stay in the car and you can treat him.'

'We can both go in. Two heads are better than one, and if he's going to go into fibrillation or do anything dramatic you might be necessary anyway.'

And that was something to look forward to, Holly thought with a sigh. They dressed hastily, grabbed their coats and were over at the Evans's house within ten minutes of the call. Mrs Evans opened the door, clearly worried sick, and pulled them both inside.

'He's in the kitchen, sitting in the big chair. He says it's the only place he can get comfortable and he's terrified to keep walking about in case he damages his heart.'

They went through to the kitchen and there they found their patient sitting at the table in a big wooden carver with his elbows propped on the table, looking haggard. His colour, Holly noted immediately, was good. Not too high, not cyanosed and blue—nothing out of the ordinary at all. He wasn't even pale, although he looked drawn with pain.

Dan pulled out a chair beside him, sat down and took the man's blood pressure, pulse and temperature while he asked him about this recent episode of pain.

Holly listened, watched and came to the puzzling conclusion that whatever was wrong with him was nothing to do with his heart or lungs or gastric system but entirely mechanical.

'Mr Evans, have you been doing anything heavy over

the weekend?' Dan said, just as she was about to ask the same thing.

'He cleared out the shed,' Mrs Evans supplied helpfully. 'On Sunday afternoon. Why?'

Dan raised an eyebrow enquiringly. 'I just wondered if it was mechanical,' he offered. 'Dr Blake, what do you think?'

'I was just going to say that. A rib, sternum or thoracic spine problem caused by strain. It could be a pulled intercostal muscle—that would hurt on exertion and on breathing in, and would give a feeling of pressure over the sternum if it was near the attachment of the rib to the breastbone. Or it could be a dislodged rib—that would fit with the postural problem and all the other symptoms as well.'

Dan nodded. 'Yes—yes, it could well. Mr Evans, can you take your dressing gown and pyjama jacket off, please?'

The man stripped, wincing when he pulled the sleeves off the left side, and as they turned him into the light Holly noticed a tiny bruise just coming out on the front of his chest next to his sternum. It was over the attachment of a rib, and when Dan pressed it gently it was tender.

'Bingo. I think we have your problem. Did you lift anything heavy?'

'No—'

'The garden roller.'

'But I didn't lift it, I pushed it and dragged it.'

'That would be enough,' Dan said. 'Right, I think you need to see an osteopath and get that manipulated, and I think you'll find your problems resolve almost immediately. In the meantime, I'm going to give you some anti-inflammatory tablets to take with food three times a day and some anti-inflammatory gel to rub on the affected area, again three times a day, and with any luck you should find it starts to settle down in a few hours.'

'But what about my heart?'

Dan smiled reassuringly. 'Mr Evans, there's nothing wrong with your heart. It's fine, and, as long as you take care of it, it will continue to be fine. If you're worried about prevention come and see the nurse and get her to tell you about diet and exercise for a healthy heart. I think she's even got a video she can lend you. Are you in a private health scheme, by the way?'

Mr Evans nodded. 'Yes—company policy so we can arrange any treatment to be at a convenient time. They found it was cost-effective and who am I to complain? Why?'

'Because you should be able to recover the cost of the osteopathy, depending on the scheme. Check with the osteopath when you ring. There's a good man in Holt—ring the surgery in the morning and Julia will give you the number.'

They left the relieved Mr and Mrs Evans, and on the drive back to the cottage Dan said, 'So, what made you think of a rib?'

'He was just too well to have anything wrong with his heart. He looked uncomfortable, but not ill. His colour was too good and, as you say, he's not fit. He's the ideal candidate for a strain. He's probably lucky he didn't get a hernia.'

'That'll be the next thing,' Dan said with a chuckle, and stretched back in the seat. 'Oh, well, at least he's not about to die of heart failure in the night. I feel much happier about him now we've got a definite diagnosis. Heavens, we're clever.'

She laughed with him, but then she lost her smile. 'We should have thought of it before,' she said, annoyed that their patient had suffered unnecessarily since Monday.

'I don't think so. He'd decided it was a heart condition, and so he was telling it to us in a way we'd recognise as a heart condition. If he'd just come in and said, "I've got this pain here," we might have got there sooner. Patients who think they know what's wrong can be a mixed blessing.'

They arrived back at the cottage, dumped their coats and boots and went upstairs. On the landing Dan paused, looking down at Holly through those wretched glasses so she couldn't see his eyes or read his expression.

'Are you likely to get back to sleep?' he asked hesitantly.

Her mouth curved slightly in a wry smile. 'Probably not, even if I get a chance. Why?'

His shoulders lifted in a shrug. 'Just wondered if you wanted to keep me company.'

Frustrated by the barrier, Holly reached up and removed his glasses. His deep grey eyes smouldered with heat, their message unmistakable. Her smile widened. 'I thought you'd never ask,' she said softly, and went into his arms.

Dan lay there beside Holly, staring at the ceiling and listening to the soft sound of her breathing. She was fast asleep, her body sprawled half over his, totally relaxed. A lump formed in his throat and he swallowed it with difficulty. Lord, she was lovely. So soft, so gentle, so passionately uninhibited when she was aroused.

It had been so long since he'd just had fun in bed, without feeling that his performance was being measured or judged or that he was simply there to pass the time with or scratch an itch.

He'd told Holly he didn't want to get involved, and to a certain extent it was true, but there were times, like this, when it was so good to hold someone who wanted you for yourself and not for what you had to offer. He closed his eyes but an image of Jocelyn formed in his mind and he opened them again, looking down at Holly's flawless, pale skin and driving the image away.

Her hair was spread over his chest, and he fingered the strands and wondered what it would be like to lie here with her like this when her hair was grey and her skin was lined and their grandchildren were asleep in the spare bedroom.

The ache of longing almost made him cry out. Was this the forever feeling Holly had talked about? If so he could quite see that it had driven her to abandon her long-held principles. It was almost enough to make him abandon his—almost. Not quite, though. Not even the promise of Holly's forever could override the pain of Jocelyn's betrayal and the agony of growing up in a broken home.

He couldn't put any trust in forever. It didn't exist outside the pages of women's fiction, and there was no way he was going to allow himself to be sucked in by a dream—even if it was the sweetest dream he could imagine. He knew from bitter experience that eventually there would be a rude awakening, and there was no way he was going to allow Holly to lull him into a false sense of security.

Oh, no.

Holly couldn't believe it when she opened her eyes to find herself in Dan's bed, stark naked and very comprehensively loved, at a quarter to eight the following morning.

She could hear Dan in the kitchen, talking to the dogs, and she slipped out of bed, pulled on his shirt and went downstairs. He was in his robe still, letting the dogs in from the garden, and he turned to her with a smile. 'Morning. Did you sleep well?'

She nodded, running her fingers through her tangled hair and lifting it back from her face. The shirt gaped open, and Dan's eyes were drawn to her body, catching fire again. There was something she wanted to try, something she'd read about but never done, of course. She held out her hand. 'How about a shower?' she murmured.

His eyes flamed. 'Together?' he said in a strangled voice.

'Why not?'

'Because we've only got twenty minutes.'

She smiled wickedly. 'We don't have to have breakfast.'

He took her by the hand, led her upstairs into his bathroom and turned the shower on full, then, peeling off his shirt from her shoulders and throwing aside his robe, he pushed her under the spray. His mouth came down on hers, his hand splayed on her hip and he pulled her up against him.

With a shock she realised how aroused he was, how

much he longed for this—and how much she longed for it, too. It was her last coherent thought for some time, and by the time she'd come down off the ceiling of her euphoria, dragged on her clothes, scraped back her still-damp hair and run down to the kitchen the surgery was filling up and Dan was chatting to Amy as if nothing had happened.

That was amazing. She could still feel the needles of the shower on her shoulders, the cold tiles at her back, the heated thrust of Dan's body driving hers wild with passion.

She could still hear his cry of release ringing in her ears and the harsh rasping of their breath as he sagged against her in the shower cubicle. She could hardly walk straight, let alone chat happily to the practice staff!

Did that mean it didn't matter to him? Was it possible it had so little effect on him that he didn't feel knocked sideways by it?

And then he looked up and saw her there, and he lost his train of thought and forgot what he was saying, and Holly knew he was every bit as poleaxed as she was. She gave him a knowing smile, flashed a grin at Amy and sauntered into her consulting room, leaving him still floundering for his words.

Her first patient was Joel Stephens who had come to have his stitches taken out. They had been in just over a week, and Holly was pleased to see that the cut had healed to a fine, clean line that would fade to leave only a very faint scar. She cut the ends of the suture, pulled the very fine thread through the length of the wound and held it up for him to see.

'There you go—all done.'

'Brilliant,' he said with a smile. 'Didn't hurt at all. You've done a good job on that.'

'All in a day's work,' she said with a smile.

'I gather you and Dr Elliott saved Mrs Peake's life the other day. Funny, you know, how people don't like her. I always found her a nice woman. She and her husband were very good to me when I first moved here with my parents. I did odd gardening jobs for them in the holidays, and she always gave me something to eat and drink and paid me well. I was glad when I heard she was safe home.'

Holly smiled. Not as glad as I was, she thought to herself. . .

Jeremiah Sproat's funeral was on Friday morning and, instead of the icy cold and biting wind of the past week, the weather had turned mild and wet, the rain coming down in sheets and drenching them all.

Holly, Dan and Phillip Blake stood at the edge of the gathering, huddled together in the driving rain, and when the old man had been lowered to his final resting place Phillip turned to them.

'Fancy coming back to the house? I've got the others covering me this morning so if you've got a deputising service organised you could sneak a little free time.'

'Who's there?' Holly asked.

'Just your mother. Why?'

She grinned. 'Dan's afraid of the boys. He calls them the Rottweilers.'

Phillip chuckled at Dan's discomfiture. 'They been giving you a hard time?' he said sympathetically. 'They just think the world of their little sister. They get a touch over-protective from time to time. You don't want to pay any attention to them.'

Dan laughed mirthlessly. 'I'll try not to.' He looked at Holly. 'Want to go back to see your mother? If you do I could get a taxi back to the practice.'

'That's silly. Come too. We needn't be long, but it would be nice just to say hello.'

Dan, not at all sure that it would be nice to say hello to a woman with the instincts of a bloodhound, wondered if it was obvious to everyone else how he and Holly had spent the night.

After the episode in the shower she seemed to have lost her shyness, and last night had been something else. He could still see the faint trace of whisker burn on her upper lip, and he knew there was more of the same on the side of her neck. Would her mother know what the marks were?

And, if so, would she be furious with him, or would she simply settle down in the middle of her web and wrap them round in the silken strands of wedding plans?

Dan felt a cold, tight panic settle over him. 'I think I'd rather go on back to the practice. You go with your father—I'll catch a lift with Joel and Mr Simpkin.'

He turned on his heel and left them there, and Holly's father turned to her with a thoughtful expression on his face.

'He's looking cornered.'

Holly nodded miserably. 'I know. I noticed. I wondered how long it would take.'

'Things pretty serious between you, then?'

Holly looked up at her father's concerned eyes and felt her own fill. 'Yes,' she said with a little sigh. 'Unfortunately, yes, they are. Do you know what I found out this week? His ex-wife is living with his father.'

Phillip's brow creased. 'You mean he's giving her accommodation?'

'No. I mean she's living with him as his partner. Sharing his bed.'

'Dear me.'

'Quite.'

'No wonder he's wary.'

Holly gave a snort of laughter. 'Wary isn't the word for it. He's fine until you mention that dreaded four-letter word, then he just panics.'

'And you've mentioned it?'

She sniffed and tilted her face into the rain so the tears wouldn't show. 'Oh, yes. Couldn't keep my mouth shut, could I? I thought he ought to know.'

Phillip slung his arm round her shoulder and led her away from the graveside. 'If it's any consolation I think you're right. He should know. I don't hold with all this feminine artifice and trickery. Your mother's never indulged in it but I've heard of plenty of women who have, and after his wife pulled a stunt like that I think the only approach with Dan has to be the direct one. He needs to know where he stands.'

'But I don't think he believes me. He said it's just because it's good— Well, never mind what he said.'

Phillip hugged her gently. '*Is* he good to you? I know you haven't had a lot of experience, and it's a difficult thing for a father to deal with, but if he's hurt you or used you—'

'Dad, put the guns away. He's wonderful to me. He just won't tell me he loves me.'

Phillip patted her shoulder. 'Give him time, love, give him time. He can't help but love you in the end. In fact, judging by the look of panic on his face, I'd say he loves you already, but he just won't admit it.'

Holly tipped her face up to his. 'You don't think it's too soon to know how I feel?'

'How long is it? Nine days? Ten? I knew within minutes with your mother. You either have it or you don't. Come on, forget about him for a moment and come and have a cup of coffee and a bit of Christmas cake. I've been wading through it but without help I think the damn thing's going to last for ever.'

So Holly went back with him and ate two slices of cake and chatted to her mother about the New Year's Eve party in the village hall and how much they had raised for the community coffers. She told her a little bit about what she had been doing this week and then, before the conversation could grow too personal, she escaped and went back to the practice.

Mrs Hodges found her in the kitchen. 'I've just made Dr Elliott's bed,' she told Holly, 'and it was a dreadful mess. I suppose his father being ill's upset him again and made him all restless. I hope he isn't having those awful nightmares again like he did after his accident. Still, at least you keep your room nice and tidy and make your bed so I can't grumble.'

Holly made a noncommittal noise and escaped before Mrs Hodges said anything else about the state of Dan's bedroom. She busied herself with putting notes from her night calls onto the computer to keep the records up to date. When there was no more 'busy' work to be found she spent the rest of what should have been an afternoon off walking the dogs and enjoying the rain as a change from the freezing cold.

She saw Becky just getting out of the car by their house, and went and chatted to her and to her mother.

'She's tons better now, thanks,' Mrs Rudge said with a smile. 'Still got that awful cough, but without the whooping. That was what scared us so much.'

'Well, I'm glad she's better,' Holly said, ruffling the little girl's blonde curls.

She continued on her walk, coming back over the fields behind Church Farm where Mr Simpkin, Julia's father, farmed. She waved to Joel and was invited in to see the milk tank where he had cut his head, and the two dogs had a romp with Mr Simpkin's collie and had to be rounded up after they went in a ditch.

'I'd better take them home and bath them,' she said to Joel with a laugh and, whistling up the dogs, she put them back on their leads and towed them home. By the time she got there she was splattered from head to foot because Buttons, by far the worst offender, had shaken himself and hurled all the muddy ditchwater out of his coat and all over Holly's.

Dan met her at the door, his face a picture, and without a word of censure took the young scamp upstairs and hosed him off in the bathroom.

Her bathroom.

By the time Dan and the dog had finished the walls were spattered, the floor was drenched and Dan was nearly as wet as the dog.

Holly sat down on the floor and laughed at him, and he threw a soggy towel at her. 'May I remind you,' he said stiffly, 'that it wasn't me that took the dogs out and brought them back filthy?'

Then Buttons shook himself again, and Dan's attempt at haughtiness bit the dust.

'I think we'll leave Rusty to clean himself up,' he said, making a strategic withdrawal to his own bathroom. 'Sort that lot out, could you, Holly? I'm going to have a shower before my evening surgery.'

So she wiped down the walls, washed the bath out, blotted up the floor and gave Buttons ten minutes of entertainment with the hairdryer before she put it safely out of the way and took him down to Rusty, who by now had licked himself clean and was curled up asleep in his basket.

Then she went back upstairs, had a quick shower in her rather doggy bathroom and emerged to find Dan back in the kitchen, grabbing a cup of tea before he went back into the fray.

'I'm starving,' he muttered, poking about in the fridge. 'I wonder what Mrs Hodges left us?'

'Steak and kidney pudding with carrots and broccoli. I'm not sure I can manage it after my mother's Christmas cake. I had two huge chunks.' She shot him a look. 'You should have come—you would have liked it.'

'Hmm. I'm not sure it would have been worth it.'

'It's a good cake.'

He laughed softly. 'It would need to be.'

She watched him go and wondered if he would ever stop running from himself. With a sigh she poured herself a cup of tea, put her feet up on the kitchen table and tried to decide what to wear for dinner tomorrow.

Not that she had a tremendous choice. There was a rather pretty dress she was fond of but it wasn't very smart, and the only smart things she had were more suitable for interviews or business lunches or right off the other end of the scale in the party range.

Then there was the cream silk dress.

Hmm.

*   *   *

They walked into the restaurant, tucked away in a quiet street in Holt, to be greeted by the owner who ushered them in, took their coats and showed them into a quiet little sitting room. There was a log fire crackling in the grate, with chairs and sofas arranged in intimate groups around it. Another couple were sitting in the corner, their heads together, and apart from that Dan saw that they were alone.

Their host brought them drinks, set a bowl of nibbles down on the table in front of them and left them with the menu.

Dan ignored it, turned to Holly beside him on the little sofa and ran his finger over her bare shoulder. He was still a little stunned by the change in her, not sure if it was for the better and yet mesmerised by her loveliness for all that. 'Do you have any idea just how beautiful you look tonight?' he murmured, scanning the elegant line of the dress with its single strap and demure neckline that managed for all that to be outrageously sexy.

'I bought it ages ago and I've never worn it. Do you like it?'

'Like it?' He laughed softly. 'Oh, Holly, "like" doesn't even begin to touch it. You look wonderful.' She did. Classy, expensive, beautiful. It was the sort of dress Jocelyn used to wear.

He banished the thought as unworthy, but it crept back over and over again during the course of the evening until he began to wish she had worn almost anything else.

Not that she didn't look good in it because she did— she looked stunning. It was just that he'd almost managed to convince himself that Holly wasn't like that,

that she didn't bother about clothes or fashion or the bright lights, and here in front of him was evidence to the contrary.

She was just the same as all the rest, he thought despondently. She might be a much nicer person than Jocelyn, but she still wouldn't be happy locked away in Norfolk for the rest of her life with him and his scars, both emotional and physical.

He was a lousy catch, and this beautiful, elegant, glittering woman would lose interest in him in no time.

Why hadn't he died in the accident? What twisted hand of fate had thought to keep him alive to torture him with this goddess? So near, and yet so far.

He would take what fate gave him, though. That was the only option open to him. He would pretend to be happy and take what she offered, and store it up against the rainy day he knew was coming.

And so he smiled and parried her verbal thrusts and ate the food that tasted like sawdust, and when the taxi took them home he took her up to his room, peeled her out of the dress and made love to her with a desperation he was sure she must feel.

Then, when she was sleeping, he crept down to the surgery, shut himself in his consulting room with a bottle of malt whisky and drowned his sorrows. He hadn't cried since he was a child, but now he wished he could because for two pins he would have put his head in his hands and wept for the love he could never have and the woman he was sure to lose. . .

CHAPTER TEN

HOLLY wasn't quite sure what had happened, but after that night things with Dan were never quite the same. Not that he had ever been easy to get close to, but now there was always some emotional distance between them, even in their most intimate moments.

She felt as if he were holding her at arm's length, keeping her out of reach of his feelings. Was it because she'd told him—yet again—that she loved him? She and her mouth. She'd crowded him before he'd felt ready to deal with it, saying those three little words too early in their relationship.

But she did love him, and nothing he could say or do would change that. She'd just have to prove it to him.

She continued to work alongside him at the practice, and eat with him in the evenings, and sleep with him at night except when it was very busy. Then sometimes she'd go back to her own bed rather than disturb him.

It also helped to put Mrs Hodges off the scent because there was no way Holly was admitting to the woman that she was sleeping with Dan. An old-fashioned country woman, Mrs Hodges would have had heart failure if she'd known what went on while Dan's sleep was disturbed!

It wouldn't have been so bad if they'd been engaged, or if they'd known each other for months, but Holly knew other people would have difficulty justifying their relationship after such a short time.

To take her mind off Dan she buried herself in her work, taking more than her share of the night calls and covering the vast majority of the weekends.

'You're doing too much,' Dan said to her at the beginning of her third week. 'I want you to do only every other night.'

'But you do the evening emergencies,' she argued, 'so it's only fair. Anyway, think of the cost of the endless taxis.'

'Stuff the cost,' he said inelegantly. 'I don't want you cracking up under the strain.'

Holly sighed. 'I won't crack up,' she promised. 'I'm as tough as old boots—'

'And I'm a monkey's uncle. You need sleep—and you're not getting it.'

'Whose fault is that?' she snapped back, and then immediately regretted it when she saw the look on his face, but the words were out and there was no way to get them back. 'Dan, I didn't mean that—'

'No, you're right,' he said tightly. 'Perhaps you should sleep in your own room when one of us is on call.'

'But I don't want to—'

'Tough. You need to be rested and on the ball for the sake of the patients, never mind yourself—and so do I, come to that.'

'And what about us?' she asked softly. 'Don't we matter too?'

Dan sighed, but went mutinously quiet and refused to discuss it any further. That night when Holly went up to bed after a call it was to find that Dan had gone to bed and his bedroom door was firmly shut.

It wasn't locked. It didn't have a key.

Nevertheless the message was clear. He didn't want her. No doubt he'd been trying to tell her that in all sorts of ways for ages but she had no experience of affairs—she didn't understand the protocol and jargon.

Hurting desperately, she went to bed on her own and lay there and stared at the ceiling while the hot salty tears ran down her temples and soaked into her hair as she wondered what she ought to do now.

Should she stay or should she look for another job? Dan needed her, but if she was making him unhappy perhaps he'd be better without her. He could always advertise for another person.

Maybe this time someone would reply.

She looked grim the next day. Her first night of proper sleep had done her no good at all, she thought, staring at herself in dismay in the bathroom mirror. Pale, pasty, her eyes red rimmed and shadowed, she looked like a refugee.

Make-up, she decided five minutes later, was a wonderful thing. She went down to her surgery and smiled blithely at her patients and wondered how many of them would have guessed she was breaking her heart.

Mr Evans, the man with the rib, certainly gave her an odd look. She smiled even more brightly, though, and asked him how he was.

'Oh, the rib's much better, thank you,' he replied, forgetting about Holly. 'The osteopath gave me several treatments and it's completely cured. That's not why I'm here—well, it is, but only indirectly. He's found something on my back and he thinks I should have it looked at—I wondered if you could tell me if it's all right or if it needs removing.'

He peeled off his shirt and showed Holly a mole. 'He reckons it's changed since I've been seeing him, and he thought it was worth checking up on.'

Holly looked at the small, apparently innocent mark on his left shoulder blade. It had a darkened edge, and looked as if it was beginning to spread from that edge. Certainly it was something that needed checking out, and she told Mr Evans that she'd like him to come in for a skin biopsy. 'When would you be able to come?' she asked him.

'How urgent is it?'

She lifted her shoulders. 'Not desperately, but we might as well get on with it. I think I'd like Dr Elliott to have a look at it as well, if you don't mind. Could you hang on? I'll just get him.'

He was between patients, by coincidence, and she asked him to come in and look at the mole. As he moved away from the desk the harsh light from the window showed the pallor of his skin and the deeply etched lines that bracketed his mouth. Thank God for make-up, she thought. At least *she* could hide behind it.

It was encouraging, though, to see that Dan also looked rough.

He followed her back into the other room, greeted Mr Evans with a smile and checked the mole, lifting his dark glasses to see it better. 'Hmm,' he said, resettling the glasses on his nose. 'Yes, I think that should come off and be sent for analysis. I'm confident that whatever it is it's in the very earliest stages of change, but I don't think we want to leave it. I tend to take all moles off now, regardless, because it's such a simple procedure. When can you come in again?'

'Whenever. I'm not working today, if that's any good.'

'Come today, then. I've got the nurse here and we've got one or two other minor surgical procedures to carry out so we may as well fit you in too. Three o'clock?'

Mr Evans nodded, and Dan left to go back to his patients.

Holly finished her surgery and went out on the calls, coming back in time to discover that Amy had gone home with a stomach upset and she was assisting Dan in the minor surgery clinic that afternoon.

Their first patient was a man with a sebaceous cyst on the back of his neck, just at the hairline. Dan explained to him what he was going to do and the man signed the consent form, an essential before they could carry out any invasive procedures. While Dan scrubbed Holly injected the area with local anaesthetic.

Once the skin was numb Dan carefully cut down to the cyst with a scalpel, freed the outside of the sac with tweezers and the judicious use of a blade and removed it whole, before putting in three tiny stitches to close the incision.

While he worked he explained what he was doing so that the patient could understand the tugging and snipping that was going on just behind his ear.

'What's caused it?' he asked as Dan was finishing off.

'Just a blocked duct from a sebaceous gland—one of the lubricating glands for the hair. Lots of people get them and sometimes they don't cause any trouble but sometimes, like yours, they become infected or leaky and then it's best to remove them.'

'Well, it certainly didn't hurt,' their patient said with a smile.

Dan returned the smile with a slight twist of his lips. 'We aim to please,' he replied, and sent the man on his way twenty minutes after he had come in with instructions to keep the site dry for forty-eight hours and come back the following week.

Next was a routine removal of the sides of an ingrowing toenail, which Holly found made her feel just a little bit queasy. She'd never liked surgery, and had gone for general practice because it didn't involve a great deal of it.

Unfortunately sore toenails were one of her worst things, and it was just typical that Amy should be away for this one, she thought ruefully. Coupled with the lack of sleep, it was almost more than she could cope with and she was only too relieved when the man limped out, his bandaged toe protruding from his sock like a trophy.

'Are you all right?' Dan asked curiously.

'I just hate toenails,' she confessed with a little shudder.

He grinned. 'Me, too.' Then his smile slipped and he looked longingly at her. 'You look tired.'

'I am tired.'

'I'll get the deputising service to cover tonight so we can both get a decent night's rest.'

'Together?' Holly said quietly.

He didn't reply. His mouth tightened, and he called Mr Evans in and excised the mole that they were both almost sure was a malignant melanoma. Holly hoped they'd got it in time or it might turn out that the man's fear, in a perverse way, had not been groundless.

The rest of the day went quickly and, as promised, Dan got the deputising service to cover the practice from midnight. She came in from a call she had gone out to at half past eleven to find that Dan had gone to bed.

As before, though, his door was shut, and it seemed that he really did intend for them to sleep.

The silly thing was, Holly thought, that she slept better with him than without him.

They stuck it for over a week and then one night, as she came up the stairs, she found Dan standing in his bedroom doorway.

Wordlessly he held out his arms, and with a sob she fell into them and hugged him.

'Hey, steady on, you'll do my ribs in like Mr Evans,' he said breathlessly, and she released him and stepped back, riddled with guilt.

'Did I hurt you?' she asked, searching his face with her eyes. But he was smiling, his mouth tilted teasingly, the left side not quite as high.

'I'll live,' he murmured, and drew her back into his arms. 'Come here, I've missed you.'

She'd missed him, too, more than she could say or dared to admit, but she was with him now and she didn't intend to waste a second agonising over what they'd lost. Without another word she lifted her mouth to his.

'Dr Blake? I don't suppose you remember me—I'm Gill Partridge. I had a baby on New Year's Day.'

'That's right. Come in.' Holly pushed back her chair and stood up, going round to admire the baby girl. She was gorgeous, and Holly felt a stab of longing that she had never experienced before. Almost like jealousy. How extraordinary. She went back to her chair. 'You must have come for your six-week postnatal check.'

'That's right. She was six weeks old yesterday. I couldn't make the usual clinic this week because I had a dental appointment, but I didn't want to wait until next week—well, it's Valentine's Day on Saturday and I thought I'd give Sam a treat.' She gave an embarrassed little laugh. 'Seems silly, really, but I didn't like to try making love without getting checked.'

'I'm sure you won't have a problem,' Holly assured her. 'You had such an easy labour and straightforward delivery there's no reason why you shouldn't be fine.'

She examined Gill and confirmed that all was well, and checked the baby over, too. She was lovely, right on target and clearly doing well on her regime, and Holly sent them away for their Valentine's Day celebration with an idea forming in her mind.

Perhaps she should plan a Valentine's Day treat for Dan and cook him a meal and seduce him, then propose to him in a weak moment. It wasn't a leap year but, then, she had never been hidebound by tradition, and she had hopes that things were improving between them. He had been quite different since their reconciliation, although he still insisted that she should sleep when she was on call and so wouldn't make love to her even though he did now allow her to stay in his bed.

What Mrs Hodges made of it Holly neither knew nor cared. She was much too worried about dealing with Dan's emotions to worry about the housekeeper's finer feelings.

Anyway, she was a sensible married woman, she knew these things happened.

So Holly planned and plotted, organised the deputising service for the weekend and went shopping in Holt on Friday morning after her calls. She bought chicken breast fillets, because even she could make a creamy sauce with chicken to serve with jacket potatoes and salad, and she found a nice bottle of sauvignon blanc to go with it, as well as some red candles and heart-shaped ramekins to make sinfully rich dark chocolate mousses.

Her plan was to send him out for a long walk on Saturday morning after surgery so she could make the mousses and prepare the salad. She might even cook the chicken if there was time so all she had to do was heat it through.

The salad, she thought, was a bit optimistic because the past week had been bitterly cold again and the ground was like iron. The pond behind the church had frozen solid again, and she noticed that the children were skating on it after school as they had at New Year.

Young David had been out there, the boy who had cut his leg, flirting with danger and apparently never learning his lesson. Holly wondered what some people were thinking about not warning their children of the dangers of ponds. It had been all right at the beginning of January but now it wasn't nearly so cold, the ice wasn't nearly so thick and the danger was much greater.

Still, she couldn't worry about that. She brought the shopping in, hid the ingredients behind other things in the fridge and rushed to her clinic. That was followed by evening surgery, and apparently endless calls that kept her going all night.

By the time Saturday morning came she was shattered so Dan took the surgery for both of them and left her lying in bed with a pile of professional journals to browse through.

She turned to the jobs at the back, just idly curious

to see what was advertised, and her eye was caught by a very familiar-looking advertisement. She read it twice, and a third time, then threw back the covers, dragged on her clothes and marched downstairs. The second Dan was out of his surgery she was going to tackle him about it! How dare he advertise her job without mentioning it to her? And why did he want anyone else, anyway?

Unless he wanted to get rid of her and didn't think he could say anything without having a replacement lined up so they didn't have to work out her notice with a difficult atmosphere. . .

She slumped down at the kitchen table, a sick feeling of dread filling her. Was that it? Did he want her out of his life? It hadn't felt like that last night when she'd crept back into bed at four o'clock and he'd taken her in his arms and warmed her up with such tender thoroughness.

She was confused, and hurt, and angry. How could he do it? Didn't he realise she'd find out? Or was that the idea? Perhaps he wanted her to find out indirectly because he was too much of a coward to confront her.

Well, he was going to damn well confront her—and very shortly.

She heard the surgery door close, heard Dan's farewell to Julia and then he came into the kitchen and smiled at her. 'Better now?' he said cheerfully.

'Better? Why should I feel better?' she said, her voice carefully controlled. 'Because I've found my job advertised?'

His hands stilled in the middle of filling the kettle, and he turned off the tap and put it down. 'Ah. I was going to discuss that with you.'

'Too damn right you were! This is my job we're

talking about. Don't you think I have a right to know about it being taken out from under me?'

He sighed heavily and came and sat down opposite her. 'Of course you do.'

'So explain, please.'

He fiddled with the salt and pepper for a moment, then took a deep breath and let it out with a rush. 'Look, Holly, I've felt for some time that this isn't working. We're both too tired because we're trying to juggle the practice and our relationship at the same time, and there aren't enough hours in the day to do either of them justice. I thought if you had another job somewhere else, we could still see each other—'

'But not live together. Not sleep together, and wake up together. That's the trouble, isn't it? It's too cosy for you, isn't it? And you like it, and that's freaking the hell out of you!'

He stood up abruptly. 'I'm taking the dogs for a walk,' he said tightly. 'We'll talk about it when I get back.'

She shot to her feet. 'I'm coming with you. There's no way you can get out of this conversation, Daniel Elliott, so don't even try.'

She tugged on her coat, put her wellies on over her slippersocks and stationed herself by the door. 'Well, come on, then.'

He glared at her—well, she supposed he did. So help her, she was going to smash those dark glasses if it was the last thing she did—

'Buttons, Rusty, come on.'

The dogs bounced round his feet, and as he opened the door they rushed out into the bright sunny morning. It felt warmer, she thought absently. Thank God. She wouldn't have to scratch the ice off the car in the night—

not that there would be any more nights if someone else took her job.

She hurried to catch up with Dan. 'Would you just slow down a little, please? We need to talk about this and if you imagine I'm going to yell about it in front of all these kids you've got another think coming.'

He slowed his strides, called the dogs back to his side and kept walking, his hands shoved in his pockets and his head tucked down in his collar. Talk about stonewalling her.

'Dan, I don't see why we can't work together. It's going fine. What we both need is more time off. You've got three and a half thousand patients on your list— that's enough for a two-man rural practice.

'If we were living together as we are, sharing running costs, the money isn't a problem. We could use the deputising service every night, if necessary, and still be well enough off. Have the emergency surgeries till midnight and from six, and get the nights covered. That way we know there's at least six hours we have to ourselves in the middle of the night. The same with the weekends—we could work one in two.'

He was silent, striding beside her, his mouth a grim line.

'What's the matter? It would work, Dan.'

'Maybe for a while.'

'Why not permanently? There are lots of husband and wife teams round the country—'

He stopped in his tracks. 'Who said anything about husband and wife teams?' he said sharply, and she could have sworn there was a note of panic in his voice.

'Well, that's what we're talking about, isn't it?' she said reasonably, trying not to push too hard. 'Living together as partners—it's the same thing.'

'This is temporary.'

'But it might become permanent.'

He gave a short huff of laughter and turned to face her. 'Holly, you're such an optimist,' he said harshly. 'When are you going to face the truth? Your forever doesn't exist—not for me, at least.'

'It could, Dan,' she promised. 'You could give it a try.'

'No. Been there, done that. Jocelyn left me, the woman I hired to share the practice left because she couldn't stand the rural isolation and she realised I wasn't interested in her and there wasn't anything else here for her—'

'But that's not me, Dan. I love this part of the world. I've lived here all my life, I've got friends and family here. Of all the places in the world, it's where I'd choose to be—and, of all the people in the world, you're the one I'd choose to be with.' She stared up into his face, wishing she could see his eyes so she could work out what he was thinking. 'Dan, I love you,' she said softly. 'That isn't going to change.'

'Holly, don't,' he said, his voice strangled. His jaw was working, and she knew she was getting to him. She was right, he did want it to work, he was just afraid to try. If she could only convince him—

There was a shout from by the pond, and they looked across to see Buttons running over the ice after a ball a child had thrown.

'He'll go through,' Dan muttered, and ran down the slope towards the pond, calling the dog towards him. 'Buttons, here, boy, come on. Good dog—'

The ice creaked and splintered, and with a yelp of

surprise the dog slithered into the freezing water.

Dan slammed to a halt at the edge of the pond and stared helplessly at the black hole in the ice. Buttons was splashing in it, struggling to get out and unable to get a purchase on the icy edge.

'Dan, you can't go in,' Holly said, holding him back. 'The ice is too thin—it's thawing. Look, it's patchy all over. God knows how he got that far across. We'll have to break it up to give him a chance to swim.'

'You're right,' he said and, grabbing a fallen branch from under a nearby tree, he started to hit the ice.

Then Holly grabbed his arm and stopped him. 'Dan, it's Becky Rudge! What's she doing? Becky, no! Get off the ice! Go back!'

'But the doggie's going to die!' the little girl cried.

'Becky, we'll get him out,' Dan promised, running round to where the ice was thickest. 'Now come here, darling, there's a good girl. Walk towards me, nice and slowly—that's it, just little steps—'

Becky screamed as she fell in, the ice disintegrating beneath her. Without a thought Dan dragged off his coat and ran onto the ice, stamping as he went to break it up. He fell through and with flailing arms he forged forwards, smashing the ice ahead of him and working towards Becky.

David was there, standing transfixed on the bank, and Holly turned to her. 'Get Joel!' she yelled. 'Tell him to bring the tractor and some ropes and ladders—hurry, David!'

The boy ran like the wind, and Holly looked around for anything she could find to help. Rusty was barking and crying and running up and down the bank, and Dan was still smashing ice and working towards the hole where Becky had fallen through.

There was no sign of the child, and as he broke through to the hole Holly heard the tractor start up and drive towards the pond. Seconds later Joel was beside her.

'I've got a long ladder—we can use it as a crawling board to get out there. I'll tie it to the back of the tractor so we can tow it out.'

He turned the tractor round and backed it up to the pond while Holly grabbed the ladder off the forks at the front and dragged it round to the pond. Hands grabbed the ladder from her and pushed it across the ice towards Dan, and then Becky's mother was there, screaming and trying to get out to them.

'No,' Holly shouted at her. 'You mustn't go in! Dan will get her.'

'My baby!' the woman screamed. 'I have to get my baby.' Holly held her arms and dragged her back out of the water.

Dan disappeared under the water, came back up again, gasping, then went under again. He was looking for Becky, Holly realised, and held her breath until he came up again.

'He's got her,' someone shouted, and as they watched Dan heaved a soggy bundle out onto the ice by the end of the ladder. Joel was on his stomach, face down and almost in reach of the little girl, and with a superhuman effort Dan picked her up and threw her into Joel's arms. The ice creaked and shuddered, the ladder slipped and then someone was in the tractor, driving it slowly forwards—towing Joel and Becky to safety.

Holly let go of Mrs Rudge and sank down on the

edge, her legs useless. They were safe. Thank God, they were safe—

'Where's the doctor?' someone yelled. 'He's gone back under!'

Ice-cold fear sliced through Holly. Dan! How could she have thought he was safe? She ripped off her coat and ran into the icy water, smashing through the broken ice down the path Dan had made. The cold stripped the feeling from her limbs and set her chest in concrete so she couldn't breathe. Her lungs were paralysed, her mind numb and her only thought was that she must reach Dan.

'On your left,' someone shouted. 'He's on your left!'

She spluttered and turned and then, floating face down just a foot away from her, she saw Dan's body. She grabbed it, seizing him by the scruff of the neck and dragging him up into the air.

A rope snaked out towards her over the ice, and she grabbed it and twisted it round her wrist and hung on to Dan. She felt hands on her body, dragging and carrying her out of the water, but there was nothing that would make her let go of Dan, nothing that could have prised her fingers out of the collar of his shirt until he was safely on the bank beside her.

Then she collapsed beside him, pushing at him and yelling at him to wake up—to open his eyes and talk to her.

His lids flickered, and then she was staring into those gorgeous grey-blue eyes, wide awake and alive.

'Holly?' he rasped.

'Yes—thank God you're alive,' she whispered, choked with relief.

'Becky?' he mumbled.

'I don't know. I'll check. Stay here.'

She staggered to her feet and crossed over to where a cluster of people were hovering round the little girl. She pushed through them and fell to her knees at the child's side. Mrs Rudge was holding her and sobbing, and the crowd were eerily silent.

Holly took Mrs Rudge by the shoulders and shook her. 'Let me see her,' she ordered. 'Mrs Rudge, let me see Becky.'

'She's dead!' the woman keened.

'She may not be. Let me see.'

Mrs Rudge straightened up, her face streaked with mud and tears, and looked at Holly. 'Her heart's stopped.'

'I can probably start it. It's called the diving reflex— it's a sort of hibernation. Everything shuts down.'

She put her fingers against the carotid artery in the child's neck and, sure enough, there was a tiny pulse, very, very slow but there.

'She's alive,' she said. 'Move back, everyone.'

She tipped the child's head right back, breathed into her mouth to inflate her lungs and then pushed five times firmly two fingers up from the bottom of her breastbone. Another breath, then fifteen pushes because she was working on her own. And suddenly she wasn't. Dan was beside her, taking over the breathing, and they were working side by side—five pushes, one breath, five pushes—until at last the child coughed, rolled over and started to breathe by herself.

'Wrap her in coats—all of you, take your coats off,' Holly said to them, and as someone draped a coat over her shoulders she realised she was shuddering and trembling with cold and reaction.

She turned to Dan. 'All right?' she asked him. He

was slumped beside her, resting on his hands and knees, his hair filthy and spiked, his face streaked with mud and a blanket round his shoulders. The one coherent thought she had was that she could see his beautiful grey eyes and they were alive. She started to cry, great huge sobs that wrenched her chest and tore her throat and did nothing at all for her elegance, but she didn't care. All she could think was that he hadn't drowned after all, and nothing else mattered.

'Shh,' he murmured, 'it's all right now.' He reached out his hand and cupped her cheek. She realised that the noise she could hear was an ambulance siren, and then her face was being swiped by a wet, muddy tongue.

'Buttons?' she said incredulously.

'He's fine. He scrambled out,' someone said.

Holly slumped down again beside Dan and stared into his eyes, and then an ambulanceman was wrapping her in foil blankets and they were being bundled into the back of the ambulance and whisked off to hospital.

'What about the dogs?' Dan said hoarsely.

'The dogs are fine. They're being taken care of,' someone assured them. Holly didn't bother about anything else after that. She leant against Dan, closed her eyes and let everyone else take control.

It was hours before they arrived back at the cottage. There was a note pushed through the letterbox from her father to say that the dogs were fine, Buttons was none the worse for his experience and he would return them when Dan was ready for them.

'I'll ring him in a minute,' Holly said.

They wandered into the kitchen, feeling a little lost and aimless. 'Coffee?' Dan said quietly.

'Mmm.'

They were both subdued. Coming so close to death was a bit hard to deal with, Holly was finding. She really thought she'd lost him, and the terror she'd felt until he'd opened his eyes would be with her for the rest of her life.

She sat down at the table, and there in front of her was the advertisement that had caused all the chaos. She looked up at him bleakly. 'We never did finish discussing my job,' she told him.

He swallowed. 'You could have died, coming in after me,' he said flatly. 'Why did you do it?'

·'Because I love you. What else could I do?'

'You might have died.'

She gave an uneven little laugh. 'So what? Without you what have I got to live for?' Her eyes filled and she dashed the tears away angrily. 'You think just because that bitch didn't have what it takes to stick at a relationship and make it work that nobody else could either. You think everyone is so superficial that they couldn't love you because you've got scars and you're a grump and you can't trust anyone, but we aren't all like that.

'You hide behind those damned glasses and you don't let anybody in, and you're lonely and wretched and you bring it all on yourself. Frankly, I reckon you deserve everything you'll get,' she finished, and burst into tears.

He let her cry. She needed the release from emotion it would bring, and once she'd settled down he'd talk to her. Until then he just made her a hot drink and sat down and waited.

'What are you looking at me like that for—and why haven't you got your damned glasses on?' she growled.

He smiled. 'I lost my glasses in the pond,' he told her.
'Good. I hated them.'

'I know. I'm sorry. I just wanted to hide, as you said.'
He dribbled a bit of salt on the table and pushed it
round with his finger. 'Look, Holly, about your forever
feeling.'

'Don't tell me it doesn't exist!' she stormed.

'I wasn't going to. I was going to tell you I've got
it, too, but I'm really afraid to trust it. I'm going to have
to, though, because if there's one thing I've learned
today it's that you're the only thing in my life that's
decent and good and worth having, and I can't let you
go. I thought I could. I thought it would be easier to
live without you and see you occasionally and let you
go bit by bit, but I can't do it. I want you here, with
me, by my side twenty-four hours a day, and if I have
to bite the bullet and marry you then I suppose I'll
have to.'

Holly stared at him. 'Is that a proposal?' she said
crossly.

Dan's heart thudded in his chest. Don't tell me she's
going to refuse, he thought in panic. 'Yes,' he said,
forcing the word out through lips that were
suddenly stiff.

'Well, damn you, Dan Elliott, I was going to do that!'

'What?'

She yanked open the fridge door and showed him her
little stash of goodies. 'I was going to make you dinner
tonight, with candlelight and music and wine, and I was
going to propose to you—and now you've gone and
done it for me!'

'Why tonight?' he asked.

She rolled her eyes expressively. 'Because it's

Valentine's Day, you fool!' she shouted at him. 'It's supposed to be romantic, and then you go and try and kill yourself and finally come to your senses and ruin my surprise!'

Dan grinned. He couldn't help himself. She was all mad and steamed up, and it was finally sinking in that she loved him still and was just letting rip because she'd been scared. Well, he'd been scared, too, more scared than he'd ever been in his life, when he'd opened his eyes and realised it was Holly who'd rescued him, but *he* wasn't yelling.

Instead he reached out and reeled her in, pulling her onto his lap, and caught her furious face between his hands. 'Is that a yes?' he asked softly.

'Yes, it's a yes! And don't you dare ever question my love again!'

He smiled. 'I wouldn't dare.'

Her anger folded like a damp tissue, and she looked down into his eyes, her own doubtful. 'You've forgotten something,' she told him.

'I love you.'

She slumped against him. 'Finally,' she murmured.

The phone rang, and she slid off his lap and picked up the receiver. 'Hello, Dr Elliott's surgery,' she said.

Then she turned and looked at Dan, and smiled. 'No,' she said. 'I'm sorry, the position's just been filled—for ever. . .'

MILLS & BOON®

Medical Romance™

COMING NEXT MONTH

HOME-COMING
by Margaret Barker

Everything changes, and when Alice returned to Ceres she had to admit that Nick's change from boy to man was definitely a change for the better.

MIRACLE BABY
by Lilian Darcy

Jenny prayed for a miracle to save baby Teresa's life and then William Hartman arrived, the answer to her prayers.

ALL THE CARE IN THE WORLD
by Sharon Kendrick

Nancy's intentions were good—she would keep her relationship with Callum on a strictly professional basis—but they were proving difficult to keep.

DOUBLE TROUBLE
by Margaret O'Neill

Looking after twins single-handedly was enough to put anyone's life on hold, but James was determined that the time had come for Kate to live again.

Available from WH Smith, John Menzies,
Martins and Tesco

ARE YOU A FAN
OF MILLS & BOON®
MEDICAL ROMANCES™?

If YOU are a regular United Kingdom buyer of
Mills & Boon Medical Romances we would welcome
your opinion on the books we publish.

Harlequin Mills & Boon have a Reader Panel for
Medical Romances. Each person on the panel
receives a questionnaire every third month asking for
their opinion of the books they have read in the past
three months. Everyone who sends in their replies
will have a chance of winning ONE YEAR'S FREE
Medicals, sent by post—48 books in all.

If you would like to be considered for inclusion on
the Panel please give us details about yourself below.
All postage will be free. Younger readers are
particularly welcome.

Year of birth...............................Month..........................

Age at completion of full-time education.....................

Single ❑   Married ❑   Widowed ❑   Divorced ❑

Your name (print please)...

Address...

....Postcode ....

Thank you! Please put in envelope and post to:
HARLEQUIN MILLS & BOON READER PANEL,
FREEPOST SF195, PO BOX 152, SHEFFIELD S11 8TE

Karen Young

SUGAR BABY

She would do anything to protect her child

Little Danny Woodson's life is threatened when
he witnesses a murder—and only his estranged
uncle can protect him.

"Karen Young is a spellbinding storyteller."

—Publishers Weekly

1-55166-366-X
AVAILABLE NOW IN PAPERBACK

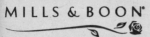

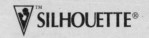

SPECIAL OFFER £5 OFF

FLYING FLOWERS

Beautiful fresh flowers, sent by 1st class post to any UK and Eire address.

We have teamed up with Flying Flowers, the UK's premier 'flowers by post' company, to offer you £5 off a choice of their two most popular bouquets the 18 mix (CAS) of 10 multihead and 8 luxury bloom Carnations and the 25 mix (CFG) of 15 luxury bloom Carnations, 10 Freesias and Gypsophila. All bouquets contain fresh flowers 'in bud', added greenery, bouquet wrap, flower food, care instructions, and personal message card. They are boxed, gift wrapped and sent by 1st class post.

To redeem £5 off a Flying Flowers bouquet, simply complete the application form below and send it with your cheque or postal order to; **HMB Flying Flowers Offer, The Jersey Flower Centre, Jersey JE1 5FF.**

ORDER FORM (Block capitals please) Valid for delivery anytime until 30th November 1998 MAB/0198/A

Title ....Initials ....Surname ....

Address..

....

....Postcode ....

Signature...Are you a Reader Service Subscriber **YES/NO**

Bouquet(s) **18 CAS** (Usual Price £14.99) **£9.99** ☐   **25 CFG** (Usual Price £19.99) **£14.99** ☐

I enclose a cheque/postal order payable to Flying Flowers for £......................................or payment by

VISA/MASTERCARD ☐☐☐☐☐☐☐☐☐☐☐☐☐☐☐☐ Expiry Date............/............/............

PLEASE SEND MY BOUQUET TO ARRIVE BY........../............/........

TO Title ....Initials ....Surname ....

Address..

....

....Postcode ....

Message (Max 10 Words) ....

....

Please allow a minimum of four working days between receipt of order and 'required by date' for delivery.

You may be mailed with offers from other reputable companies as a result of this application. Please tick box if you would prefer not to receive such offers. ☐

Terms and Conditions Although dispatched by 1st class post to arrive by the required date the exact day of delivery cannot be guaranteed. Valid for delivery anytime until 30th November 1998. Maximum of 5 redemptions per household, photocopies of the voucher will be accepted.